Prehistoric Tales - Volume I

Chris L Adams

Chris L Adams

Copyright

Dear reader,

Whether you purchased this story or received it as a gift or as part of a promotion, in reading it you are investing something as valuable as the money you or another may have spent for it--your time. So, thank you so much for taking time out of your busy life to read this story.

If this is an eBook, it is for your personal enjoyment, so please do not give it away to others. If you would like to share it with another, please purchase an additional copy for each recipient. If you suspect this book has been pirated, consider going to your favorite retailer to purchase your own copy; it's the honest thing to do. That way, you will make it possible for me to write more books, because I'll have to worry less about how to make ends meet.

Thank you for respecting my hard work. Now, have fun with the story!

Chris L Adams

Introduction

If you're familiar with my stories you know that I enjoy writing pulp-style tales like those created by my favorite authors of the pulp era who wrote for magazines like Argosy All-Story Weekly, Weird Tales, Famous Fantastic Mysteries and others.

Having spent a couple of years rewriting my epic Barsoom saga where I converted three lengthy novels that weighed in at a half-million words into a multi-volume series, and also completing *The Banshee of the Atacama* after having started and stopped on it a half dozen times since I began writing it in 2016, I needed to clear my head by focusing on something completely different.

For several months I'd had recurring thoughts about a prehistoric man who is banished from his tribe and in the course of his wanderings, encounters someone quite different from himself. This story is the culmination of those thoughts.

At about the same time that I was pondering this story, I began working on a new painting. That happens whenever I'm between paintings and I watch a few Bob Ross episodes; I find him so inspiring. That painting, titled *The Lair*, eventually became the cover for this story--a first for me. The painting is tied to and has influenced the story, and since I worked on both simultaneously, elements of the story ended up in the painting, as well.

I hope you enjoy reading this romp through the Pleistocene. Alright, and maybe a couple of other places. But it is a *Bizarre Tale*, so that should be expected, right?

Chris

Contents

1. Fire-Feeder

Through slitted eyes, Bru--a hunter of the Seven Rivers tribe--glared at Gla as his hated rival descended out of the hills bearing the head of a saber-toothed tiger. Despite the fury the sight triggered, one side of Bru's mouth curled in scorn as the stout hunter witnessed the more-slightly built man struggling to carry his grisly burden.

Gla was one of the tribe's fire-feeders, a station typically filled by the weaker among the tribe because--well, after all they weren't good for much else. Yet for all his fragility, and inability to defend her or even hunt for her, Gla had only the day before proclaimed his interest in winning the hand of Oona, sole daughter of Ra, the chief. Suspiciously--at least to Bru, anyway--this proclamation came right on the heels of Ra's announcement that the mating price was to be the head of Tysk, the tiger.

Bru turned and stalked off in the direction of his hide shelter with his teeth clenched so tightly that it quickly caused a nerve to begin leaping beneath one eye. Coming unexpectedly upon Fra, a youngling of the tribe, Bru shoved him, causing the juvenile to fall down. He kicked at him, as well, but missed when the rangy youth scampered away on all-fours.

Why did the fire-feeder venture out that morning? It was not required of his kind to forage for the grass and mammoth dung they burned to maintain the Sacred Flame; this was done for them by the fuel-gatherers whose only job was to hunt for fodder for the flame. Yet there was no arguing the fact that Gla, a timid, raily youth bearing neither scar nor bruise, set out that morning only to later return--still without blemish--bearing the one trophy that Bru coveted with every drop of his life's blood.

Although his own, keen eyes were the first to spot Gla staggering beneath the burden of almost half the scrawny youth's weight in saber-tooth head, Bru's discovery was almost instantly followed by others. In Bru's wake the entire tribe began crying out in acclamation of Gla's surprising conquest and valor, with none questioning how such a feat could have possibly been accomplished by one so unversed. And now Gla would reap the spoils that every unmated man in the tribe desired to claim for his own.

As Ra's daughter began ripening into the curves of womanhood the requests for possession of her increased significantly. Initially, the chief, her father, thought to allow Oona to have her pick among the young bucks who wished to mate with her and demand for himself only the standard dowry of food or weapons--or in the case of such a beauty as Oona, both. Well it was, tho, that he had not spoken too quickly. For to his muddied intellect was birthed inspiration conceived in the coitus of avarice and opportunity.

Ra happened to witness two men negotiating for the same tusk, each vying with the other in his offer to the tusk's owner, causing the chief to become consumed with the idea of setting a higher price than typical on the head of his daughter--and that price would be the skull of Tysk.

It was an unheard of price for a female. Saber skulls were difficult to come by; those of the tribe who possessed them were seasoned hunters who were already mated and who would not part with their saber skulls on their lives. For, were these not proof of-- and later a source of--bravery and prowess to those who hunted in the hills?

Bru had flown into a rage when he learned of this unexpected price to mate with Oona. Whosoever would possess the girl must first brandish the head of Tysk. If ever one might have benefited from the vocabulary that the dim future was destined to inherit it was Bru on that day. Yet his peoples' tongue was simple, and they knew not the manner of cursing as would their civilized descendants. There was little wonder, then, that he struck Fra, the rangy youth; for emotion must find its expression or one will go mad.

Bru embarked on a hunt two years before, led by Ra. They didn't have any luck that day and, ranging farther than normal afield, were caught after sundown far from the shelters of the people. Not wishing to attempt to return home in the dark, they camped in the hills--squatted, really--determined to resume the hunt at dawn. In that cold, dark camp Ra revealed that ever since he was a stripling, he had desired the skull of Tysk, the fanged one.

Bru sensed that this childhood desire had become an obsession for the chief; that Ra wished more than anything to possess a tiger skull so he could set it beside that of a cave bear and a giant wolf that Ra's father harvested as a young man, these skulls having become Ra's after his father was trampled to a pulp by Moosh, the mammoth, on an ill-fated hunt. Bru could still hear Ra's disembodied voice, coming out of the pitch black of night, grumbling about never having had the opportunity to harvest a tiger before youth and vitality fled his limbs.

Stomping through the snow, Bru arrived at his shelter; roughly forcing aside the heavy pelt that was strung across the opening, he entered where he could seethe in private.

"Bru should have Oona!" he swore. "Bru should kill Gla! Then Gla can't buy Oona!"

It was an empty threat and he knew it; but it felt good to say it. Men--hunters and otherwise--were highly valued by the various tribes--plainsmen, hillmen, forestmen. The tribe would die out but for the women who prepared the food and manufactured all sorts of things, including tanning the hides of the beasts that their men would bear to the camp; children, of either sex, were the life's blood of the tribe.

To slay any of these was an offense not to be undertaken without the expectation of dire consequences for the hothead. But one of Bru's type--powerful, capable, prideful--are ever prone to bluster, even of things they cannot actually do, or which they know to be foolhardy.

The man squatted, leaning for a short while against the center pole of his shelter. His eyes fell upon piles of newly made weapons and freshly smoked jerky; the sight caused him to grimace. After a few moments of this, having decided that doing something was better than sitting in his shelter doing nothing, he leaped to his feet and headed back toward the center of the tribe's collection of shelters where he learned calamitous news that was not entirely unexpected.

"Gla will mate with Oona!"

The first man Bru ran across grinned and said this to him in their simple tongue which consisted of as many hand signs as it did barked syllables.

"Who says Gla will mate with Oona? Bru will bring a skull! Bru will mate with Oona!" Bru's brows met in the middle of his forehead from the sheer intensity of his frustration, while the tick under his eye leaped even more vigorously in its antics.

The other man, a seasoned hunter who already possessed a mate, a brood of tough youngsters and a tiger skull--and who recognized in Bru's words the rashness of youth--barked a harsh laugh. "Where is this skull, Bru? Still on the shoulders of old Tysk? Ha-ha!"

Others within hearing also scoffed. With his blood boiling from the course taunts of his fellow hunters, Bru stalked aimlessly through the collection of hide shelters, kicking stones and throwing sticks at youngsters who found they had good and immediate reason to stay out of Bru's path. When a mother glared and came after him, though, Bru ducked his head in shame and hurried away.

Had those who ridiculed him been less in number, Bru fumed, he would have thrown them to the ground and stomped their teeth into the backs of their jaws! He would have pulled their ribs apart and thumbed their eyes into their sockets! As it was, he stalked away in grim silence; but his fellow tribesmen's guffaws followed him relentlessly.

Bru was angry; and mostly--if he admitted it--he was angry with himself. After he became Oona's secret lover at the onset of winter the hunter had dissuaded the girl from immediately announcing news of their impending nuptials because he wished to put into effect a plan that he felt would eliminate all of the certain competition he would have for her hand. Now he wished he'd listened to her and staked his claim then. Ra would have been forced to reveal his secret price, and Bru might have harvested a tiger in time.

Instead, Bru had been secretly accumulating the standard price for a chief's daughter. He had assembled a collection of finely crafted weapons of stone and obsidian--each made by his own hand and unused. In addition to the spears and knives he'd fashioned were the tanned hides and smoke-cured strips of jerky which he intended to conveniently have on-hand when he announced his intentions to the girl's father. It was these things which sat in his shelter. They were useless to him now and he couldn't stand the sight of them.

Bru's plan called on his staking his claim only a month prior to the Wyrm Moon, this being the shortest duration prior to that moon phase that one could stake a claim for the daughter of a chief. At that point, he was sure no one would be able to match or exceed his amassed offerings; they would not have enough time.

Or they shouldn't have been able to!

Naturally it was not well received by the hunter when Ra unexpectedly announced the non-customary price of a saber-tooth skull--which Bru was currently unable to pay and which rendered moot all his months of clandestine effort. It certainly wrought havoc with Bru's short temper that it had not been he who brought the cat's head before the chief. Instead it was a rival--and one of the cowardly fire-feeders, no less--who did so and who found favor with the chief, where Bru had not.

While he was in the act of squeezing between two shelters, Bru was suddenly and roughly grasped by another.

"Bru! Follow me! We go to prepare the pot for the Skull-Rite!"

Bru's heart pounded in his chest as though it would burst through his ribs at mention of the ceremony. "Skull-Rite?"

"Bru simple, Skarf smart; Skarf teach Bru! Gla bring Tysk's head. Tonight, we boil Tysk. Tomorrow, Gla pay mating price. Gla ready to make the beast with two backs with Oona! Ha-ha! You pretty stupid, Bru! But now Bru knows how things work! Now--go that way!"

Bru preceded Skarf. He had little choice to do otherwise; although Bru was in possession of an envious, athletic build, Skarf was a much larger man and would have beaten him to a pulp if he tried to flee. Bru's time was running out. Although per the tribe's laws fair Oona must await the rising of the Wyrm Moon--signaling the end of winter--before she could take a mate, this specified phase would occur in only a matter of weeks.

1

0

At that time would Tuzu shed her soft, nocturnal light upon the by-then melting snows. Only then might be celebrated the mating rites as befit the daughter of a chief. For, only the daughters of chiefs are mated on this sacred night, and upon no other night might they be mated. But, per the laws, prior to that, the first who paid the price would secure the girl for his mate.

Staggering beneath the ponderous weight of the hollowed-out skull of an enormous mammoth, Skarf, Bru and two other men bore the grisly object toward the center of camp. With one of the tusks biting painfully into his shoulder, Bru experienced to the full the insult of having to bear the very pot that would soon be used to boil Tysk's head so that Gla could claim his victory prize--that being soft, dainty, beautiful Oona.

Blackened by years of use by the tribe for their various rites and celebrations, the skull was heavier than a mammoth skull had any right to be. This was because it was layered with clay to prevent fire from coming into direct contact with the mass of bone. The inside of the skull had been similarly layered, with new clay bedding being added when it was discovered that the skull would no longer hold water.

With the immense pot finally cradled in its holders--a framework of heavy mammoth bone which supported the tusks and the rear of the skull--Bru slipped away before Skarf could direct his recruits in the gathering of burning materials. For the Skull-Rite demanded a larger supply of burnable fodder than what the few fuel-gatherers could be expected to accumulate by themselves.

That very night, the revered skull having been made ready, the *Sacred Flame* would be used to kindle the fire to life beneath it. Soon, the time would draw nigh when the saber-tooth's head would be boiled to clean the bony mass--an orgy the tribe called the Skull-Rite--which would make of the tiger's skull a potent thing of magic and power. And while the severed head was bobbing in its boiling bath, the tribe would chant and sing and eat in celebration of the coming rituals.

2. The Skull-Rite

"How all Bru's plans wrecked in one day?" mused Bru. Only that morning had he and Oona trysted. While the bulk of the tribe were hunting, checking traps at the lake's edge, or gathering dung and grass with which to feed the *Sacred Flame,* the girl went in secrecy to her lover's shelter. Then later that same day Gla entered camp bearing a saber-tooth head. And now--or rather, tonight--the tribe was to perform the first of the rituals of the mating of a chief's daughter. There was nothing left that could go wrong.

The boiling of Tysk's head--the execution of the Skull-Rite--seemed rushed to Bru. Perhaps it was only his own desperation speaking, but it caused him to become highly suspicious of Gla and even more jealous if that was possible. With the spring moon still weeks away, why the hurry to perform the ritual? Was Gla that anxious to lay with his soft, new mate? Bru frowned; when he thought of it like that, he could understand why Gla would wish to rush things along.

Maintaining a hide shelter between himself and Skarf as best he might so that his fellow hunter might not see him slipping off, Bru rounded a structure only to come unexpectedly upon one of the tribe's fuel-gatherers. The man was headed toward the camp center where smoke, rising into the air, was indicative of the imminent revelries.

Fuel-gatherers worked in conjunction with the fire-feeders. But where fire-feeders like Gla rarely left camp, fuel-gatherers were dedicated to ranging afield in search of the necessary fodder to feed the *Sacred Flame.* Although they carried weapons of defense--for theirs was, after all, a world of constant danger--they were only rarely forced to use them, knowing as they did the terrain where one might encounter the great predators and steering clear of them. In Bru's estimation, they were only a trifle higher in social order than the fire-feeders--but not by much.

"Prud," he said distastefully when he saw the man who was yet another stick-of-a-man that the hunter might have snapped in-half like a dried twig. Bru was a heavily muscled young man with little

1

use--and no respect at all--for stick men. "Gla is no hunter. How did Gla slay Tysk, huh?"

The hunter, his chest and arms swelling in youthful vigor and wrath, took a truculent step closer to Prud, causing the other to lay his hand on the pommel of what looked like a freshly crafted obsidian dagger thrust through a hide strap tied about his waist. Volcanic glass was found near the foot of the mountains across the lake which was well within Prud's foraging radius.

"Gla slay Tysk with spear!" Prud said. He seemed proud of the accomplishments of a member of his caste--or, close to his caste at any rate.

"What spear Gla use?" Bru pressed, eyeing the other narrowly. Bru raised his empty hands, palms up. "Gla has no spear!"

"Gla used his father's spear! Bru stupid! Bru not hear Gla's story. Tysk fall on spear. Gla cut off Tysk's head!" Prud said.

"With what? His teeth? Gla carries no knife! Gla needs no knife. Gla is a coward!"

"Gla take head with father's knife," the other said, weakly.

Bru noticed that Prud was looking everywhere except straight into Bru's eyes. He distrusted men who wouldn't look him in the eye when they spoke to him, unless there was a good reason for it-- such as when the hunters whispered to one another in the reeds while keeping their eyes peeled for game. The slighter man seemed awfully determined on defending Gla, in Bru's opinion. It took a few moments to matriculate through Bru's slightly muddled intellect, but he was beginning to suspect some form of collusion between the two--Prud and Gla.

"Why boil Tysk tonight? It not Wyrm Moon."

It was Prud's turn to eye Bru accusingly. It was public knowledge that the hunter had intentions for the daughter of Ra, although none knew exactly how close the two had grown. Knowing he risked a physical encounter if he pushed the hunter too far, the fuel-gatherer could not resist the temptation of rubbing it in the face of Bru that a smaller, less physically-imposing man would soon possess Oona.

"Go right now, hunt Tysk! Go get your own skull!" Prud grinned. "Gla will mate with Oona; nothing Bru can do!"

Bru planted his fist in the middle of the other's face and stalked off to find Gla, leaving Prud lying senseless in the snow behind a hide shelter. But Gla was not at his shelter when the hunter arrived. With red murder in his heart, the hunter made his way next to the shelter of Oona. But he did not find the man there, either--which was a good thing for Gla.

"Bru will show Gla!" the hunter muttered, crunching over the frozen ground. "Bru will show Ra! Bru will show tribe! Bru will go now and slay Tysk!"

The hunter could not have said whether it was the memories of Oona's entwining limbs that goaded him the most, or the thought of losing her to a weakling--which he found particularly galling. For a long time, he stalked about the nearer hills, but never once did he come across the spoor of Tysk. This was probably a good thing because the evening had matured to dusk and Bru could not see well in the dimming light, while Tysk could.

Darkness was rapidly falling upon the plains; a partially obscured moon glinted across the surface of the slushy lake and reflected from snowpacks in the frozen heights of the mountains. The sounds of revelry came to Bru distantly from the camp which was eerily illumined by dancing firelight.

"Gla!" Bru roared his frustration aloud into the emptiness of the night that surrounded him.

Dejected, he made his way back to the encampment where he found his nemesis holding the offending head aloft in preparation to dropping it into the cauldron beneath which scorching flames roared orangely and crackled musically. Garg, the shaman of the Seven Rivers Tribe, an old woman, was shaking a piece of bone with the knuckles of some animal tied to it with pieces of sinew, chanting mystically and sprinkling herbs that she alone could identify into the bubbling cauldron.

Ringing the mammoth skull, the tribe chanted and laughed while hotly glowing embers hurled skyward. Tribesmen with globs of jiggling flesh on the ends of fire-hardened sticks roasted meat to cram into their already-stuffed bellies. Oona was standing beside

1

her father. In the hunter's eyes her great beauty was magnified by the leaping flames which caused her to glow with a rosy warmth Bru found intoxicating and maddening.

Motivated by the heart-wrenching sight of his lover looking so desirable in the leaping firelight and of her soon-to-be betrothed reveling in his triumph, Bru glared through a red fog as his contender prepared to consign the skull to its bubbling doom; and he snapped. Charging upon Gla despite the efforts of others to stop him, and before any could realize his intent, he laid hands upon the severed head and wrenched it with little effort from the feeble grasp of his challenger, knocking both Gla and old Garg to the ground in the process.

Almost instantly Bru observed something about the grim prize that went unnoticed by the others, and which his scrawny rival would wish to destroy all evidence of before it might be observed by any rivals for the hand of Oona. The thing Bru glimpsed was a discharge leaking from one half-opened eye which was oozing in a slow-creeping runnel down the tawny hide of the beast's fur on one cheek.

To Bru, this indicated but one thing--putrefaction. In the dim intellect that lay between Bru's ears, it came to the savage hunter that the beast had been dead for quite some time--days, weeks; months even. Gla could not have slain Tysk with a spear that day!

For, did a thing rot instantly? Given the snow covered plains upon which they were presently encamped, the nearby icy hills and mountains, the glaciers visible in the heights, he knew they could not. Although a simple man, he knew that a thing that died while the snow was on the ground might still be eaten in the spring--so long as there were no warm days between the time it perished and the time it was consumed. Already they'd experienced a warm day; this was how they knew Wyrm drew nigh.

Bru knew that the thick ooze on the cheek of the dead tiger was decomposition and guessed that the tiger died the previous fall. It had begun to rot but became frozen by the onset of winter and had only recently, with the increasingly warm weather of approaching spring, begun to thaw; somehow, the fire-feeder had discovered it.

Or had its whereabouts been made known to Gla by another? Bru jerked his head in the direction of Prud who was standing close by.

One final thing was proof to Bru beyond all doubt that the beast had perished at some point in the past and not that morning, and that last piece of evidence became his when he shoved the grisly thing into his own face and inhaled deeply ere rough hands were laid upon him and the severed head was hastily snatched from his grasp by the conferees of Gla. Corruption! Corruption filled Bru's nose as water does a hollow spot when a rock is pulled from a muddy shallow. Rot--filthy, stinking, rank, reeking, rotten decay.

Before any other might lay a hand on the skull, Gla--the severed head having been returned to him by Prud--dropped it with a s*ploosh* into the boiling pot without further ado from which steaming depths it would later be dragged after it had been boiled white and clean. The hair and flesh-filled water would then be poured out with the rest of the tribe's waste. None would ever know of Gla 's deception--none, that is, but Bru who found disfavor the instant he snatched the trophy from his rival.

"Gla did not kill Tysk! Tysk is rotten!" the hunter shouted.

"What did Bru say?" asked the mate of Skarf.

"Bru is jealous," Skarf nodded sagely. "Bru thinks only Bru can kill Tysk! Bru thinks Oona should be Bru's!"

"Stupid Bru! Bru stupid!"

Skarf shook his head and nodded at the same time.

None minded the hunter when he cried foul. He was instead pummeled, dragged to his own hide shelter, and trussed to await punishment. None minded him, that is, save for fair Oona who preferred her brawny and courageous Bru to the shorter, skinnier, less-daring, less-handsome Gla.

In the village center behind the hunter the festivities continued--without Bru.

3. Banished

As Bru lay bound in his own shelter Oona entered secretly through the rear entrance in the use of which she'd grown accustomed in recent months; she wasted no time untying her lover. In the dimly lit interior, while the tribe reveled about the bubbling pot into the small hours, and while the elders discussed a fitting punishment for the rash hunter, the youths railed against their ill-fortune when they were not lavishing upon one another their feverish affection. Their speech, limited by the surrounding darkness because a portion of their language consisted of hand signs, was quietly whispered; later, they slept.

Before the young lovers knew it, dawn found them. Awakened by a gentle glow filling the shelter, they found their passions kindled anew. In the midst of their lovemaking, however, came the sound of many feet crunching through the freshly fallen snow that had been visited upon the plains during the night. Ere the girl could slip out the way she had come the tanned hide covering the front entrance was drawn aside; the first face to appear in the opening was that of the girl's father--Ra.

As Bru, dripping in the profane sweat of his passions, rose to his full height from between the soft limbs of Oona he expected to die. To those who came suddenly upon them it mattered not that he and the girl found favor in one another's sight, and that with favor was born affection, and with affection had grown the physical entwinement that follows naturally on its heels.

"Oona! I gave you to Gla!" the chief roared; his speech was a mixture of grunted syllables and hastily formed gestures.

The girl cried out as her father wrenched her from Bru's side. Yet Bru could do nothing; what might one do against five leveled spears?

The chief turned his angry gaze upon Bru. "Bru disrupted the Skull-Rite! Bru knocked down Garg! Bru knocked down Gla! Bru profaned Tysk! Gla killed Tysk--not Bru! Gla brought Tysk's head--

not Bru!" Ra stabbed a finger in Bru's face, and that finger shook in the immensity of the chief's wrath.

Bru shrank a bit at mention of Garg, the shaman. That was an unfortunate accident which he heartily regretted. He was fond of Garg, having known her since he was a child. But when he thought of Gla, Bru punched the center post of the shelter--a long sweeping mammoth tusk--so powerfully that it caused snow to start from the shelter's slopes and the leveled spears to flinch.

"Gla did not slay Tysk! Gla does not even hunt! Tysk's skull was filled with rot but Ra does not care! All Ra cares about is the skull!"

Finally, he'd found the opportunity to tell the chief of his discovery. The night before none would pay him any heed. Now perhaps Ra would become resentful of the trick being perpetrated upon the tribe and punish Gla. Several of the gathered hunters flanking Ra smirked then, or chortled, as was each's inclination. Bru started getting a sinking feeling.

"Why you scoff? Why you always mock Bru?" he asked.

"Bru young and dumb," snickered Skarf. "It doesn't matter if Tysk dies from spear or drowns or falls off a cliff! Tysk's skull is all that matters! Skarf found Tysk's skull in the lake! You a dumb-dumb, Bru! Ha-ha!"

Bru didn't bother replying. He was securing a hard lesson in the ways of the older generation. Perhaps he was naïve as Skarf suggested; he held romantic notions where he imagined himself harvesting a saber-tooth, or a cave-bear, in an epic, honest hunt; the cutting off of the head and bearing it into camp as a sign of one's conquest; the boiling of the skull in the mysterious rite oversaw by their shaman that would imbue the whitened bone with the magic that would later infuse the hunter with the skill and power and courage of the beast he had so heroically reaped.

Now he was beginning to see that this was not the way of things at all; that these men were happy just to possess the skull despite how it was acquired--even one filled with rot and decay.

"Skarf right!" Ra roared. "Gla bring skull! Stupid Bru! Skull of Tysk has power. That is all! Skulls don't know how they die!"

Although his rival was one of those standing in the shelter, Gla hung behind the hunters who crouched on either side of Ra. But it was Ra's gaze that Bru met; the others, including Gla, did not matter to him.

The sneer of contempt on the hunter's face spoke eloquently of his feelings relative to Gla and the keepers of the *Sacred Flame*--kept burning day and night by the fire-feeders whose job it was to nurse the living fire lest it die. In Bru's mind fair Oona deserved the mightiest that the tribe had to offer--not the weakest; and certainly not a conniving worm like Gla.

"Fire-feeders don't even forage for the moss and grass they burn!" Bru accused, stabbing a finger at his rival. The huntsman ground his teeth in recollection of Gla bearing the severed saber-toothed head into the camp. Perhaps if Ra understood that Gla could never protect the girl as could Bru he would reconsider this ill-matched union.

"Gla is a coward! His fingers smell of dung! If Gla ever met Tysk he would go to fill Tysk's belly--" he started to argue.

"Shuttup!" Ra's roar would have frightened Kusk, the bear, from his den. "Bru should die!" Ra physically forced himself to calm down before he spoke again, but before he finished his voice began to rise again in volume. "Ra hunted with Bru's father. Ra hunted with Bru, son of Bru. But Bru betrayed his chief. Bru is banished!"

And one finger of Ra, shaking with boundless rage, was stabbed toward the rear of Bru's shelter which sat on the outer periphery of the tribe's collection of shelters perched below a glacial lake south of the mountains. On the other side of that wall of hide lay the wilderness; grim, cold, lonely. Bru had been cast out.

4. Into the Wilds

At Bru's back was his own hide shelter where it sat on the outer edge of the camp. Before him were the snow-covered plains, the hills, the rivers and the lake; beyond that were the mountains. Standing between the shelters and spilling onto the plains was the entire tribe down to the young ones and nursing mothers. It had been years since one of their own had been banished as this was a rare occurrence that happened but infrequently; curious, they all wanted to watch.

The last tribesman to be banished had been a deranged man called Plith who went crazy several years before and randomly killed two tribesmen with a stone ax. Bru, a youth at the time, discovered his remains later; Plith's body bore the evidence of having been ravaged by Haas, the Great Eagle and further gnawed by Kusk, the bear. There hadn't been much left of him, but Bru recalled recognizing a few tattered and rent pieces of clothing.

The hunters of the tribe, standing between Bru and the collection of shelters, held their rough, stone-tipped spears at the ready. Bru was one of their own but none were certain what he might attempt. A desperate man might go mad with fear and attack. For this reason, he was only allowed his stone knife; they would allow him that much that he might later fashion weapons to survive in the wild. Skarf, crouched with lowered spear, expected to come across Bru's remains in the near future.

Oona stood between two hunters; her cheeks were streaked with her tears. One side of her face was reddened where Ra disciplined her. But Ra had not corrected her so much that her future mate would not want her. He'd broken no bones, having only stung her backside and her face somewhat, as he saw fit. Before any could stop her, she broke free from her chaperones and rushed to her lover's side.

"Oona loves Bru!" she cried, throwing her arms about the hunter's mighty frame. The girl trembled with uncontrollable sobbing.

His face firm with resolve, Ra motioned his men back and approached the pair alone. Seeing her father's approach, the girl hastily pulled a necklace from over her head and slid it over her lover's until it lay against his broad chest. She briefly placed one hand palm down over the little bobble depending from the simple, raw-hide strap, and then on leaden feet retraced her steps to stand between Ra's hunters, passing her father on the way but not deigning to glance at him.

Standing several steps away from the community where he could do them no harm, Bru awaited the coming of Ra who continued toward him although his daughter had already returned to her place of her own accord. The chief stopped before him; he glanced at the necklace Oona had just placed about the neck of the exiled hunter--a bit of wooly rhino horn about as long as the width of a hunter's palm. It'd been carved into the shape of two lovers clasping their arms about one another; Ra grunted.

"Ra remembers when Bru took that horn; Ra never knew what Bru did with it," he said.

That was because Oona always kept the bauble hidden, like their relationship. Bru grimaced.

"Rhut, the rhino, charged without warning that day." They both knew the story but Bru told it again anyway. "Bru was in its path, using his knife to clear a way through the brush. The hunters were behind Bru; their spears were ready. Bru leaped aside into the brush, but swiped at the monster as it passed, and severed the tip off its horn. Bru found the horn in the brush. Skarf killed Rhut. Skarf kept Rhut's skull; but Bru kept his portion."

Ra nodded; this was all true. Bru, a rangy and daring youth at the time, had neatly lopped off the tip of the wooly rhino's horn, but it was Skarf who cast the spear that felled the beast. To Skarf went the honors and the skull while the meat went to the tribe; but, although he tried, Skarf could not prevail upon Ra to force Bru to hand over the tip of Rhut's horn, to Skarf's disappointment. Per Ra's decree, Bru kept what Bru rightfully took, and the same for Skarf. The chief had recognized the bravery of the youth's act.

"Ra knows Gla's skull was rotten," Bru said quietly. "If Ra waits, Bru brings a skull--a mightier skull. A skull filled with honor, not rot!"

"Yes, Ra knew! Bru can't see that Ra doesn't care! Skull is skull," Ra hissed in return, his own voice rising with rekindled rage. "Bru defied Ra! Now Bru pays! Bru goes *now*!" Not for the first time, Ra's finger pointed imperiously toward the distant lake and low hills.

Bru's expression might have made a lesser man quail, but not old Ra. The hunter started once to look a last time upon Oona but stopped himself; it would only make it harder for both of them. Without a backward glance he started off across the plains.

The hunter intended to make for the hills for it was in his mind to locate the remainder of Gla's Tysk and determine what had slain the great cat; not that it mattered. Ra's actions illustrated quite clearly that it didn't matter. But Bru wanted to see for himself whether or not the great cat had been killed with a spear, as Gla claimed. It was Gla's assertion that the spear still resided in the body of Tysk after he entered the campsite without one. Bru snorted. The claim was not only a lie but was completely unrealistic; the coward should have just admitted that he'd found the body--he would have possessed the price demanded by Ra, regardless.

"Bru! Bru!"

The hunter recognized the voice of Oona. Sobs wracked the girl's frame as Bru, his expression rigid, crunched through the snow away from the camp and the people; one hand clutched the tiny carving at his breast he had made which was of himself holding his cherished Oona.

A few hours later found the hunter in the foothills with craggy mountains towering before him. His sensitive nose sought the smell of decay, yet the freshly fallen snow aided the evasive scent to elude him.

"Bru will find Tysk," he muttered. "Bru will drag Tysk's body to the tribe. Then the tribe will know that Gla lies!"

His eyes, as always, warily sought the towering, icy peaks dominating the sky; Bru shivered. But it was not the air coming off his snowy surroundings that caused Bru to shudder. His people were plains people. Their haunts were the lowlands, not the craggy heights where nothing flourished. There it was that Haas, the Giant

Eagle, made his lair. Bru would not have admitted it to any man but the vertiginous altitudes caused jolts of fear to shoot through him whenever he approached their heights too closely. It was his belief, and that of his fellow tribesmen, that the mountains might fall crushingly at any moment.

Throughout the remainder of the day the hunter searched for Tysk's headless remains but without success; it grew late. It was never safe to walk the hills practically unarmed but walking around after nightfall with only a stone knife was recklessness beyond the pale. He should have constructed a new spear for defense first, but the desire to find Gla's headless tiger had overshadowed all else.

In a crevice between two boulders Bru sought refuge with his empty belly growling like a cave bear. He scavenged what nearby brush there was to be found, cramming it here and there to make a roof and to have something to lay upon other than snow. Upon some of this same brush he slowly chewed. It left him wanting meat--hot, dripping and charred from the touch of the *Sacred Flame;* reminded, he cursed Gla.

5.   A Dead Tiger

Awakening stiff, cold and hungry, Bru set out early the next morning, picking back up with his quest to find Gla's headless tiger. Although he now knew that Ra did not care how a skull was procured, Bru still wanted to take proof of Gla's foul ruse before the tribe. If this still failed to convince Ra to change his mind about who he would allow to mate with Oona, it would at least cause the remainder of the tribe, who would recall hearing Gla brag about how he used his father's spear to slay the tiger, to look upon the fire-feeder for the lying piece of scat he was. And who knows, the changing sentiments of the tribe might urge Ra to rethink his decision.

If his plan worked to perfection, Bru would return to the camp site with the remains of the tiger and, upon seeing the testimony of their own eyes, Gla would be the one excommunicated. That thought made Bru grin, and he continued the fantasy in his head-- of Gla sleeping between two boulders and eating dead grass; of Gla ultimately meeting Kusk the bear with nothing but a knife clutched desperately in his quaking grasp. A roughly barked laugh involuntarily escaped Bru's cracked lips.

If only he knew exactly where Gla had severed the head! Given the amount of time the fire-feeder had been gone that day, the tiger's body could not be too far beyond the lake. Skirting the base of the mountains, Bru made his way east, paralleling the shoreline.

Bru foraged while he walked, finding a few dried winter-berries the birds and bears had somehow missed. Some of them were rotted, but he ate them anyway; he mentally added rotten berries to Gla's diet in the fire-feeder's miserable, imaginary future. The way became more and more jagged and broken with rock from the mountain heights the further he progressed. The lake now lay southwest of him.

"Gla not come this far!" he grunted angrily, having caught his foot on a rock and stumbling. "Gla is weak. Bru is strong!"

He refused to acknowledge the fact that he had eaten next to nothing for two days and that privation was beginning to take its toll. As part of Bru's punishment Ra forbade him victuals. While   2 the tribe was roasting meat during the Skull-Rite the hunter was languishing in his shelter; languishing, that is, but for the attentions of sweet Oona. Having consumed only a few dried and rotted berries and some field grass in the past two days, the hunter was weakening.

Approaching a rugged canyon carved out of the side of the mountain, he made his way cautiously over the uneven rock, his keen nose still questing for the scent of putrefaction. Ah! There it was! He paused and sniffed again, taking a really deep breath this time.

"Bru smells Tysk," he grunted with satisfaction.

The hunter picked up his pace, faltering a couple of times when he went too quickly over the jagged rock and blaming his stumbling on the roughness of the terrain instead of his growing weakness. Far above his head reared The Fang of Tysk--a striking peak his people so-named for its resemblance to a tiger's tooth. He kept his eye averted from the ceiling of stone above him and continued working his way along the base of the mountain.

In moments he discovered that which he sought--the headless body of a tiger. The rear half of the saber's body lay flattened beneath a giant slab of stone that had fallen from the wall of the canyon, apparently just as the great cat was passing beneath. Or maybe the beast had made its lair here, and perished in the rockfall, being unable to flee quickly enough to escape its doom? No one would ever know. And now it lay beneath a slab of granite that weighed untold tons; or rather, half of it did.

There was not a spear in sight.

"Bru knew! Bru knew!" he nearly shouted. Although he let his voice grow louder than he intended, he had not spoken more loudly than might be heard beyond fifty feet away. Seeking for movement that might indicate the presence of one of Tysk's peers, or a member of the clan of Kusk, the bear, he was reassured when no sign of motion nor any hint of the scent of any beast other than the dead saber-tooth at his feet rewarded his questing senses; he fell to examining the corpse.

25

All about the tiger's body Bru sought a second time for the haft of a spear. To be thorough, he moved some loose stone and scooped away freshly fallen snow. There was definitely no spear haft to be found.

"Gla lied!" he spat. "Gla lied! No spear here."

The man was ecstatic to have verified his suspicions, but a part of him almost wished that there was a spear present so he might be more adequately armed. He still had not taken the time to fashion an ax or spear to defend himself with and was armed only with the stone knife Ra allowed him to take with him into exile. Continuing his examination of the site, he next found what he guessed was the very shard of obsidian Gla had used to hack off the beast's head; it was still slathered in dried gore. But it was only a very sharp shard, not a knife, *per se.*

"Bru knew Gla lied!" the hunter swore. "Brue knew Prud lied, too! This not Gla's father's knife!"

Once again might the hunter have benefited from a knowledge of the future development of Billingsgate that would occur far after his epoch. But the manner in which he danced about the tiger's corpse, the stabbing motions of his dagger hand, the stomping of his feet and the suggestive throttling of strong, curled fingers--the indications were all too eloquent. The man was getting worked up into a murderous frenzy when the dislodging of a rock around a bend down the canyon came to his keen hearing. Becoming quiet, he heard voices.

"Hillmen!" he hissed--but not too loudly.

Having only moments in which to do so he sought a place to hide. The area was covered in scattered and broken rock, but most of it was small and would not conceal him from prying eyes. He was almost to the point of desperation when he spotted a projection from the cliff face which lay directly above the tiger. He was forced to clamber upward quickly to avoid being seen and only just managed to throw himself prone a moment before a group of men stepped around the turn and headed up the canyon floor in the direction of the dead saber-tooth's body.

2

6. Hillmen!

"See? Sprig was right! Sprig smelled Tysk!"

"Sprig is not the only hillman with a nose," grunted another, sounding sullen. "Snoz smelled Tysk, too."

Sprig was a braggart who got on everyone's nerves.

The men entered the canyon and crept stealthily forward until they were standing below the projection upon which Bru lay prone. The hunter recognized them by their garb and dialect; they were members of the Dappled Hills Tribe. The hunter scowled. He had slain two of their number last summer in a raid they perpetrated. One of their number managed to capture Oona and was dragging her away when Bru ran him through with a spear. It was that very act which had precipitated his and the girl's relationship.

These were enemies of his people, coming down into the plains in the springs and summers to plunder, slaughtering what the plainsmen considered to be their herds, carrying off their women and children, killing their men. Bru decided that he would observe them for a while before determining if he should attack and kill them all now, or if he should merely watch and bear word later to his tribe that hillmen were across the lake.

It might have been that Bru, although weakened from lack of nourishment, was temporarily full of Pleistocenic optimism and braggadocio. But after taking into consideration that there were half a dozen hillmen, each of whom was armed with a spear and either a stone knife, ax or cudgel thrust through his raw hide belt, the plainsman decided it to be the better part of valor to bide his time, and then take this information to Ra, together with the body of Tysk. For he now determined that he would free Tysk's corpse and sled it together with the piece of volcanic glass that Gla used to sever the tiger's head back to the tribe as evidence of Gla's perfidy.

"Lies! There is no spear! There is no knife!" Bru whispered under his breath as he lay upon his perch. "Bru will warn the tribe. Bru will bring Tysk. Then they will see. Maybe then Ra will banish Gla. Then Bru will mate with Oona."

The hillmen were directly below him now. Immediately one noticed something that Bru hadn't considered when he was seeking a place to hide--the hunter's tracks in the snow.

"Someone been here!" a hillman grunted.

Bru's heart hammered in his chest. He wracked his brain trying to recall if he had walked carelessly in the freshly fallen snow after entering the canyon, or if he had leaped from rock to rock, from which the winds whistling down the canyon had stripped much of the fallen accumulation. Normally, he would proceed in a manner that would not bring attention to himself for exactly this reason. And then he recalled wiping snow away in the vicinity of the tiger's body in his search for the spear; Bru's heart hammered anew.

The hillmen looked about but did not see anyone. None of them, luckily for Bru, decided to climb up to examine the rocky projection upon which lay the plainsman who knew he would be killed if they discovered him. Still wary, the hillmen went back to their examination.

Above them, Bru sneered at their woodcraft. "Bru would know that tracks led in, but not out. Stupid hillmen."

Squatting now, they examined the decapitated body. One of them found the same piece of obsidian as had Bru--the fragment used by the fire-feeder to remove his grim trophy. Relieved to have so-far avoided detection, Bru's heart shrank again as the hillman picked up one of Bru's pieces of damning evidence of Gla's deceit.

"Plainsman cut off Tysk's head! Stupid lowlanders," Snoz grumbled. The other hillmen grunted in agreement; like the plainsmen, the hillmen also liked to preserve the skull of Tysk and other mighty beasts. After a moment Snoz tossed the heavy, obsidian sliver to the ground where it happened to land flatly across the edge of a large rock and shattered into splinters. Seeing nothing else of value to make them linger, they presently lost interest in the corpse and, leaving the way they'd come, continued on their way.

One of the pieces of evidence of Gla's guilt now lay destroyed beyond all redemption. Out of habit when trying not to exhibit pent rage, Bru squeezed his fists so tightly that his fingernails cut into his palms. Why had he not taken the shard with him? He laid it down while he was examining the tiger and then forgot it in his haste to find a hiding place when the hillmen startled him with their arrival. These splintered fragments would prove nothing! The crushed body of Tysk alone would have to suffice to prove Gla's deceitfulness to the tribe.

"Stupid hillmen! Good thing for them Bru too busy to fight today! And Bru still has Tysk."

With the hillmen gone Bru wasted no time in returning to Tysk's corpse. One less astute in woodcraft might wonder how the plainsman intended to lift the heavy rock from the corpse to free it for removal but this was not Bru's intention at all. Instead, the hunter began wedging and shimming several pieces of rock beneath the great slab on either side of Tysk to prevent the immense stone from settling any further. Taking up a fragment of thin, sharp-edged rock, he next began carefully removing soil and gravel from around and beneath the dead body, keeping a chary eye on the slab. He would excavate beneath the body until it could be slid from under the weight of the stone.

"Bru find wood, drag Tysk," he informed the great slab that lay atop the tiger as he excavated beneath the mouldering corpse. In his mind he envisioned the sled he would make of small saplings and woven grasses. In two days' time, he estimated, he would be back at the campsite with this obviously crushed and headless body of Tysk--much, he hoped, to Gla's dismay.

"Where is your father's spear, Gla?" he imagined asking of the fire-feeder. "Gla stupid. Bru smart. Bru smarter than Gla," he mumbled, confidently. "Gla is the dumb-dumb, Skarf will see."

The utterance he heard the next instant, coming as it did from behind him and as unexpected as a bolt of lightning on a clear day, startled Bru so badly that he jerked in surprise and struck his head on the slab of stone beneath which he was excavating. Sharp pain exploded through his skull. The instinct to survive, though, caused the plainsman to ignore the agony and leap dizzily to his feet to face his enemy--for enemy this must be since here he could expect to find none but foe, whether they went about on two-legs or four.

The figure that met his eyes was beyond Bru's simple comprehension. It was tall--much taller than Bru. It possessed two legs as did he, causing him to at first think it to be yet another hillman. But it was covered in strange skins of a smooth appearing substance unlike anything with which he was familiar. These skins were as colorful as the flowers that covered the plains in the spring after Kuzu celebrated the time of Wyrm.

For a head it possessed a bulbous, misshapen affair which the simple hunter thought most resembled an insect's, with large, bulging eyes of impenetrable black. Above these eyes were what he took to be its antennae, while below the eyes were angry looking slots where a mouth should be. It did not have mandibles, however, which was reassuring but only further confused the plainsman.

"What are you?" Bru managed, not knowing what else to say.

For answer, the other brought up an appendage from its side in which it clutched a black . . . something or another; Bru could not begin to guess what it was. The stranger leveled this thing at Bru, muttered several utterances in bug speech of which Bru recognized not a syllable and then a flash of light temporarily blinded him. He felt a sensation as though he were falling and falling and falling. He never felt his body hit the ground, though. This was because in reality he merely slumped to his haunches and then slowly leaned back against the slab laying on top of Tysk where he remained in a crouch.

For what seemed a very long time the creature walked toward him, taking a very long time in Bru's opinion until it was finally standing above him. Assuming an equally slow, drawn out crouch in mimicry of Bru's, the figure stooped to the hunter's level, reached out to him--again, extremely slowly to Bru's senses--and moved the plainsman's head back and forth from side to side, as though examining him. The creature again brought to bear the same black *thing* he had previously leveled upon the hunter, only this time it swept it sluggishly up and down Bru's body, especially about the hunter's head.

Out of the being's insectoid face unintelligible sounds emitted. To Bru, they sounded like the stranger was talking to him, but it's mouth never moved; yet the sounds persisted. The oddly outfitted figure continued to run the black thing it clutched over the stunned figure of the hunter. Mumbling to itself a near constant stream of unintelligible jargon, it finally examined the object in its hand, apparently evaluating something it could see of which Bru was ignorant. Dizzy, Bru stared, unable to move a muscle, his eyelids becoming heavier and heavier. Everything to the hunter's vision seemed to be occurring in slow motion and he could not recall ever having felt so sleepy in his life.

Bru struggled to stand but found he could not so much as move a single muscle. To his ears came the sound of approaching voices--the hillmen were returning! Terror filled his mind--to be thus helpless before his enemies, unable to rise and defend himself . . . They would kill him right where he so helplessly squatted.

The stranger obviously heard them a moment before Bru did, although the hunter found this incredible to conceive because Bru was known for his sensitive hearing. However, the colorful being had definitely risen and turned to face the oncoming hillmen a second before Bru detected their approach, causing the hunter to sense the creature was in possession of an abnormally acute hearing range; that, or Bru's hearing was being affected by his present dizziness.

"Snoz hear something!" Snoz said, rounding the eastern corner of the canyon. "Snoz hear good!" Indeed, Snoz had heard something.

The instant the six figures reappeared, the stranger leveled the bizarre contraption he clutched in his hand upon them and began sweeping it slowly back and forth. Unlike the effect it had when he used it on Bru, however, this time it caused the midsections of the hillmen to begin . . . disappearing. As roughly a foot of each torso disappeared in a misty haze, the hillmen collapsed to the ground, gasping in unspeakable agony.

Their cries continued but grew rapidly weaker; some ceased. The stranger, either wishing to spare his poor, unfortunate victims' further agony or simply being sensitive of hearing and having grown tired of their yowling, strode up to their bisected bodies and swept the upper portions of their ruined remains. From side to side he swept the contraption while Bru, still propped up by accident on his haunches against the giant slab, watched as their heads and faces turned into a gory, smoky essence most of which floated away, while some of the mist settled gruesomely to the stony soil and scattered snow drift on the canyon floor.

The hunter's lids drooped lower and lower, despite his efforts to open his eyes and focus. The creature, obviously content with its handling of the hillmen, turned and retraced its steps toward him. Bru struggled but could not move so much as a finger. His eyes closed, and he was consumed by blackness.

7. Ice Cave

Bru awakened lying flat on his back, staring up at the ceiling of an ice-rhymed cavern. Great stalactites of stone and ice depended above him; the place was cold. He was firmly attached to a surface by bindings at several points along his body of an unknown material that he could not make out from the inflexible position in which he was bound. His arms were secured at wrist, elbow and also close to the armpit. There were bonds at ankles, knees and groin; about his midriff, across his chest, about his neck, and lastly across his forehead.

Unable to move anything other than his eyes he began to panic with that dread of the unknown. He struggled, vigorously, against the bonds yet found them unbreakable. He wondered, as inflexible as the material seemed to be, that he didn't injure himself in his efforts. Maybe he actually was cutting himself and he just couldn't feel it? But his nose--which could smell a freshly slain carcass for a half a mile--did not detect the smell of blood; nor did he feel any cold wetness from his own, life's blood upon his limbs in this frigid place.

While he lay there breathing heavily from his exertions, with the freezing vapor of his breath rising above his face and temporarily blinding him with each exhalation, and stifling as best he might the claustrophobic screams that kept trying to escape his throat through sheer will (for, was Bru not among the bravest of the tribe?) the hideous head of the unknown creature suddenly appeared above him and stared fixedly down into his eyes. Seeing that the captive was awake and attempting to move, it began chattering rapidly in its unintelligible voice.

No one ever heard of an insect that spoke before, but Bru began to get the feeling that that was precisely what this thing was attempting to do--to communicate with him. But then, no one ever saw a bug this big before, either; thus reasoned Bru. Although he was fearful in such a vulnerable position which negated any attempt at defense or escape, his thoughts caused him to wonder if the smaller varieties of insects he had crushed underfoot his entire life chattered and chittered as did this, their giant relative, and they were just too small and their cries too tiny for Bru's kind to hear them?

The hunter was still lying supinely when the giant bug thrust its hideous head above him and again gazed maniacally down into his face. It then crossly uttered many more bug words as though Bru should have understood them and was at fault because he didn't. Now the creature manipulated something out of sight on the flat surface to which Bru lay fastened, his frantic thoughts assuring him that it had secured him here with some revolting, bodily material it was in the habit of excreting to hold its meals immobile until it was ready to devour them.

Bru felt the surface beneath him begin to pivot and shortly was in an almost vertical position, with the insect-like creature standing before him, towering over him in its great height; it was at least a head taller than Bru. The thing kept up a stream of non-stop chitter chatter as it went about its lair in which he could now see many unknown things that caused him to doubt the veracity of his eyes.

Pausing, the creature began fiddling with its bulbous head as though it were bothersome to it; its appendages began working feverishly along the sides and rear of its hideous skull. After a few moments, while it stood facing him, he was aghast to watch it begin pushing its head off of its shoulders using its long, tapering insect hands. Bru screamed in a horror he had not experienced since the time a flock of Edu caught him away from the tribe; they eat their prey alive.

Shortly, the bizarre figure completed the action of pushing its head off its shoulders. Standing upright, having leaned over at the waist in the extremity of its efforts, Bru was shocked to see standing there now--not an insect--but a man. For, although it still yet wore its vibrant, colorful skins, this could be nothing but a man--but what a man!

Fully a head taller than was he, the figure's features were delicate and finely crafted, more finely than anything Bru ever saw before. Hairless and smooth, with eyes as blue as a glacier river, the stranger was certainly an odd looking person, and nothing like the brutish, muscular men with which the hunter was familiar.

The stranger instantly began chattering away once more in its unknown language (in the use of which it oddly never once used its hands as did Bru's folk, although it did animatedly swing its appendages about from time to time in apparent enthusiasm or agitation), but the tone of its voice sounded natural now, causing Bru to deduce that it was the unusual, second head that had distorted its voice earlier.

Now the tall man, vivid in his striking garb made of an animal's skin with which Bru was unfamiliar, began running feverishly back and forth about his lair, twisting and flipping mysterious protuberances, causing lights to appear that looked like distant stars on unknown contraptions that defied identification to illumine and to emit sounds from seemingly nowhere that hurt Bru's ears-- unnatural sounds that the plainsman had never before heard.

Holding in one hand the device he used earlier to kill the hillmen and to render Bru powerless, the man approached the hunter. Bru felt his last moment was upon him when he saw the slight leer of disdain twisting that smooth mouth and exposing those white teeth that were whiter than teeth had any business being.

Standing before the hunter, the stranger raised his unknown thing toward him and swept Bru with its unorthodox lights. As Bru struggled to twist his head away only to find that he was still unable to move, the stranger forced yet another unfamiliar object over his head and face.

And Bru's head exploded with visions he could not yet understand--and an agony he could not stoically endure.

8. A Torturous Education

Bru wanted to die; he wanted to die so fervently that he called upon the stones and giant icicles of the stranger's lair to fall upon them and slay them both despite the fact that, being a plainsman, this was a death he particularly feared--to be crushed beneath the jagged stones of the frightful mountains.

"Bru dies!" he ripped from a shredded throat. "Bru dies! Slay Bru, mighty mountain. Kill stranger! "

These and other utterances were forced from between lips bloodied from the powerful gnashings of the tormented man's teeth and the tight clenchings of his pain wracked jaws. Agonizingly, his muscles stood out like rigid mountain ranges across the entirety of his body. And then came the flood of nausea--soul wrenching, gut twisting, flip-flopping sickness.

"Bru dies! Belly kills Bru!" he wrenched pitifully. His abdomen twisted in knots and gyrated upward toward his mouth.

The stranger, his face filled with inflexible purpose, quickly removed the first device and clapped a different one over Bru's head. Portions of the new device went down Bru's throat, further gagging the plainsman. Other sections cupped his nose, plunged into his ears and covered his eyes, leaving him in nauseous, pain-filled blackness.

Seconds later Bru heaved his immortal guts out only to feel it forced back down his throat by the thing the stranger had clapped over his head and face. His ears were stoppered such that he could not quite hear his own screams, but the images of plunging through infinite darkness, of unknown worlds and distant stars never ceased; and weird words--words whose meaning he slowly began to recognize, syllable by syllable and consonant by consonant.

Bru never understood if he was asleep and but dreamt that he was undergoing this awful torment, or if the torment was so extraordinary that it was causing him to fantasize that it was just a dream so that his mind might cope with the terrible truth--that something this horrible was actually happening to him. He realized the passage of time and that he had not ceased to have his mind

3

6

filled with such an influx of imagery and ideas since arriving in the cave as would boggle the minds of the simple people of the plains.

He was unconscious when the stranger pulled the horrid thing from his head and face, but he awoke when the chattering monster-man finished changing out the attachments. The man talked almost unceasingly, a fact which really began to irritate Bru. He was too weak to fight the attaching of the helmet device to his head--for such he somehow now understood it to be--and merely stared into his tormentor's eyes which were as chilling as a block of ice.

"O *jpir* you survive this next *ytrsybrmy*! You *jsbr* already *hpmr* farther *yjsm smu* other! You *vsidr* me to *jsbr jpir*, you *dyiiof* troglodyte!"

"I am a hunter, you beast, not a troglodyte," Bru grit in the man's own tongue before his face, eyes, nose, mouth and ears were snorkeled, probed, covered and stoppered by the unholy thing the man again pressed forcefully upon him.

A tinny crackle sounded in Bru's ear, and briefly he heard the now-hated voice of his jailer. "Good! You're learning, you *finb* brute!"

"Brute my a--" Bru gurgled around the probe. But then the sound cutoff in his ear and the torment began again. Tensing every muscle in his already tortured frame, Bru tried to force his mind to focus on something--anything--peaceful and remote from this ice-cold cavern in which he was being tormented to death.

He endeavored to conjure an image of Oona, but her beautiful face and form was instantly replaced with an image instead of the outsider's choosing. Even more horrible came the realization that when he tried to consciously think of the girl's name it was viciously nudged aside as one word on the heels of another of the stranger's language intruded on his thoughts. The only word Bru found he could mutter in his mind as his brain's tissues were being imprinted with endless streams of language and imagery--was Bru.

9. An Expanding of the Mind

Why was the outsider doing this--what did he hope to gain? The focus of Bru's instruction was now becoming more focused--not on the galaxies, suns, blackholes, dark matter, comets and other things that go to make up the expanse of deep space he'd experienced in his previous instruction, but rather of the specific planet from which the being hailed.

He learned that the man, Draugra by name, had set out from a world that his people called Xyla which was part of a group of over a dozen worlds orbiting a beautiful, blue star such as Bru had never before seen in the heavens. Having learned about the cosmic distances that existed between stars, he understood that this Xyla lay in a different galaxy millions of light-years from Bru's world which hadn't yet risen to the point where his people could talk without gesticulating hand signs--a world dominated by giant behemoths in which his people often lived in terror and awe, causing them to scamper from meal to grave.

With this latest attachment came a flood of knowledge about the stranger's home world, conveyed to Bru via the medium of the helmet-educator devices that Draugra's people invented and with which they learned all things they wished to know. They utilized the devices to educate themselves, and less frequently to educate the peoples of other, equally civilized worlds where the beings had attained a certain level of cerebral advancement.

Bru was nowhere near this minimum requirement but was rather a plainsman of the Pleistocene being force-educated with so much information that he came to grudgingly concede that the people of Xyla were among the most preeminent, sophisticated beings in the cosmos. For the last two million years they'd been working their way outward from their planet's position near the center of their galaxy in the exploration and mapping of its celestial bodies and its dark pitfalls. Their technological prowess was astounding; there existed not many questions for which the Xylans and   other worlds that supported advanced beings with whom the Xylans associated did not have answers.

3

While they greatly enjoyed the fruits of this knowledge and progression, Bru learned that in their academic expansion they had become static; that their knowledge had reached an apex; that they could devise nothing scientifically new; that their technology, which was advanced and exceedingly impressive, could advance no further without a new influx of inspiration--or a leap in evolution of cosmic proportions.

Most Xylans were content to lead lives of indolent ease for theirs was a world of great beauty and sundry pleasures; yet not all were of this mind. Their government was rattled by this cessation of development and were led by a council whose goal was to see past the stymying blockade on their intellectual advancement. Toward this end, many daring adventurers set out to scour the reaches for unmapped, life-supporting planets, when they could find them, taking particular interest in sojourning upon those rarities of rarities--unspoiled worlds peopled by untutored savages who were barely above their hairy progenitors in intellect. For it was on these infant worlds that they felt lay their greatest hope of discovering that next leap in evolution that continued to evade the greatest minds of their beyond-ancient world.

To Bru it felt as though his instruction would never cease. When it did so, it was only to repeat what came before--a swapping of one helmet-educator for another and then a new tutoring session would begin. The curriculum of this latest inculcator device was even more tightly focused than those prior, instructing Bru in all manners of language, arts, science, physics, biology, physiology, anatomy--in short, every form of study on Xyla including one called psychology which he deemed to be almost useless the instant his brain was populated with it.

As before, the exercise was filled to the brim with intolerable agony that left the hunter in tears and gagging. When necessary, his body was induced with liquid nourishment directly into his stomach via the helmet's appendages so that he never suffered the pangs of thirst or hunger, this seeming paramount to the instruction device which governed all manner of his diet, maintaining his hydration and intake of proteins and nutrients. This latest bout of tutoring lasted twenty days, bringing the tally of his absence from the plains at roughly two months to date.

***

Bru was dreaming of being home; it was the first time he'd dreamed in months. Semi-conscious, he only barely realized that the tutoring had ceased because no longer was the painful, sickening influx of information and imagery pouring into his pulsating brain tissue. Sleeping uninterruptedly for the first time in over two months (for his forced tutoring had gone on relentlessly day and night even when he was nearly insentient from the torment) he drifted over the plains of the Tribe of the Seven Rivers.

He was walking through melting snows and traversing greening, waist-high grasses. The sun was high in the sky, warming his face. He removed his tanned pelt--donned that morning to fight the chill--and slung it over one arm, no longer needing it. Over one shoulder he carried his spear and, in a hide-pouch slung crosswise over his torso were the bodies of several small creatures; he was returning from a hunt.

He entered his hide shelter and, upon seeing him, Oona, her belly filled with his offspring, smiled a wide, beautiful smile and ran to meet him; she threw her arms about her man. He had left his spear leaning against the shelter outside and now he dropped the game filled pouch to the floor. He scooped his mate into his arms, joying to the rounded pressure of her tummy as it pressed eagerly into him.

"Bru!" she cried, excitedly. "Bru greatest hunter in Seven Rivers! Bru killed all the Pooca!" She smoothed a long, dark tendril of his hair out of his eyes and back behind his ear, smiling up at him all the while with her own beautiful orbs.

"Well, not quite all of them, you silly thing!" Bru laughed lightheartedly. "If I killed all of the Pooca, they'd be extinct and then what would we do? The whole tribe would malign me for never having Pooca again! Not that I'd blame them! They make for an absolutely fantastic stew. But I'm sure we'd find something else with which to fill our cookpots. Say, did you know that the Pooca is actually a cousin of the marsupial? I never had any idea!"

Oona looked at Bru with an odd expression on her face. Without him realizing that she had inserted it, she was suddenly withdrawing her arm from deep within his throat. He had not seen her shove her arm into his mouth and down into his stomach; it just suddenly appeared there. But he was certainly aware of her slowly withdrawing it. His eyes bulged reflexively, he gagged, and then Bru opened his eyes to see the stranger withdrawing a helmet-educator from his face; the extension that was inserted into his stomach was sliding slickly out of his mouth as he came to full consciousness.

10. Draugra

The hunter, still strapped to the pivoting table, was unable to resist as the other attached various things to his body. Bru eyed his captor through hate-filled eyes. He never realized he could detest a man as thoroughly as he detested the one standing before his pain wracked body. Not even Gla rose in Bru's estimation to the heights of disdain that this other had attained. Yet after so many weeks of inactivity he was much weakened from atrophy; he doubted he could throw a pebble at the moment, let alone a punch.

"What is the purpose of these things?" he asked bitterly. Despite his weakness he struggled briefly against his bonds, albeit uselessly. The bombardment of knowledge he'd been on the receiving end of--and which would have answered the question he asked--had left his brain reeling . . . his head felt spongy; he was finding it difficult to focus; clarity, he somehow knew, would come later. The other finished attaching something about Bru's waist. A similar object already encircled Bru's forehead, and various other devices clung as if by magic to Bru's tanned and hairy hide.

Draugra released the restraint holding Bru's head to the pivoting table and for the first time in months the hunter looked down at his body. At least, he used to be hairy! What had happened? His skin was smooth now, and virtually hairless. He would be the laughingstock of the tribe! This was not how a man should look! There were females in his tribe with more hair than this.

The next thing that Bru noticed was that the necklace he'd fashioned for Oona--and which she placed over his neck with her own two hands when Ra banished him from the tribe--was now missing. Glowering, he raised his gaze to stare at his tormentor.

"Oh, for the love of Lyra would you stand still! How can I be expected to attach these devices if you continue to prance and jerk so?"

"I don't want your devices on me! Take them off!" Bru grit. "Where's my necklace?"

"Stow it, you blasted jackanape! There! Finished--no thanks to you!"   4

2

The man stepped back and surveyed his handiwork. "Your own mother might not recognize you, by Lyra. For a troglodyte, you clean up nicely. I hardly expected the extraneous hair loss though. I'll have to make note of that--"

"Call me a troglodyte one more time and I'll--"

"And you'll what, you impertinent ape? These devices prevent you from doing anything to me. Once activated, you cannot come within two paces of me without being brought to your knees. Within the confines of a single pace you'll be rendered unconscious and should you creep further than fifteen-hundred paces from my side you will be stricken senseless. That would not be too healthy considering our current elevation--can you imagine falling off this mountain and being oblivious of the fact? You're going to be here for as long as I have need of you--so get used to the idea."

The sheer, staggering amount of data that had been impressed upon the hunter was, for the time, confusing to him. But slowly, he realized what the man was saying and that he spoke the truth; he recalled seeing the schematics of these devices during the data transfer and knew them to be fool-proof against any effort to circumvent or tamper with them.

"Where's my necklace?" the hunter asked for a second time. "I had it before--"

"I removed all of your . . . things. Nasty things; I hated to even touch them. But since it seems important to you, I shall keep it and return it after we are finished--but not before."

"I want it now!"

"*Pthammit*! I said after we are finished! Now get your *pthazz* onto this conditioning device."

Draugra pointed at a contraption he'd brought forth, another device from his world, but this one featured a seat. Bru recognized it as a conditioning device from Draugra's memories, a piece of equipment that was utilized on low-gravity worlds to maintain strength, bone density and fitness. Using his handheld device to release the remaining constraints on the plainsman's body, the Xylan watched without a shred of pity as Bru collapsed to the ice-cold stone and then struggled to drag his weak form onto the piece of equipment.

"Thanks for the assist," Bru grit once he settled onto the seat, out of breath.

"You're welcome. Actually, it's proper that you should thank me. I've elevated you above the quagmire in which you previously existed and dragged you to the forefront of the pack, as it were. Good; that device will have you up and walking in no time. Lyra, this has taken long enough!" the outsider railed. "All that time I wasted on all those others--blast their rotting hides! If I had known earlier how much more adaptable the brain of the lowland type is, I would have fetched one of your kind at the onset and possibly been on my way home ere now. It must be the denser atmosphere at lower elevations; *pthakked* if I know. I've been on this Lyra-forsaken planet for almost two of your years. I was supposed to be here for a month, tops, to study the local fauna--of which you are an example!"

Bru stared at the man. He knew from his forced tutoring that the man's people were of the proclivity to sojourn on other planets for days or weeks in study or just to amuse themselves, and that they possessed the technical expertise to travel immense--staggeringly immense--distances relatively shortly, although the fuel for these vessels was very costly.

Visions of the outsider's friends, family and lovers flashed through Bru's mind. "You should have stayed on Xyla, Draugra. Whatever will Penelephii do, I wonder? No doubt Pylapharum will keep her warm at night, though."

Draugra frowned.

"You will refrain from mentioning her--do you understand? I wrestled with myself whether to use that last instruction helm or not which consists, obviously, of my own memories. Have you ever wished there were two of you? I need an assistant who is basically a double of me--but one more versed in the *phastronautics*. I made sure you were my equal in intelligence in every way possible even at the risk of your knowing information to which you have no right to be privy, *ptham* you."

"Yes, I know. Actually, I know most everything stored in your narrow head up until a couple of years prior to your coming here. There are blanks--empty abysses where I have no idea what should be there."

"Well, hopefully nothing important."

"Let me go!"

"No."

"Why not?" Bru's teeth ground reflexively.

"Having one of your empty abyss moments? I said I needed an assistant. Consider yourself a useful *phidiot*."

"*Pthak* you, Draugra. You can't call me a *phidiot* without calling yourself one. I am, after all, your equal in nearly everything--morals excepted, obviously."

"Yes, well, you'll always be a hunter-gatherer to me and a simpleton albeit one with certain know-how, admittedly. I required an associate since I can't be everywhere simultaneously. I needed one with whom I can reason out difficulties, chiefly the one in which I find myself at the moment."

"The quandary of being trapped on another world."

"I needed someone versed in engineering," Draugra continued. "And since I wasn't precisely sure what technical expertise I would require, I . . . installed all of it."

The man looked at Bru oddly then, as though he were amazed the hunter's head had not exploded from the massive knowledge dump that he'd performed on the savage.

Bru eyed the other narrowly. "Why did you not simply install the technical knowledge you required into your own head and leave mine, and those hillmen's, alone!"

"The Xylan mind may only absorb so much knowledge during the course of a lifetime. Let's just say that I near that limitation. I'm a doctor in biology and I dabble in geology. What I am not is a starcraft engineer. That's where you come in."

"Apparently, you're not much of a *philot*, either, since you wrecked your ship. I find no memories of prior knowledge of my world. So, you are trapped on a planet which no one knows the existence of because it has not yet been charted. This planet is your own discovery, then."

"You're shrewder than I guessed! Good. I need an astute man if I'm to escape here and return to--"

"Penelephii?"

"I was going to say Xyla," Draugra snapped his jaws shut and pressed a button which caused the activation of the devices attached to Bru's body.

Bru felt a subtle current come into the metallic devices; he glared. He was tempted to lunge from the conditioning contraption at Draugra to put to the test the supposed debilitating effect should he venture to approach too close. He hesitated. After two months of torture, he wasn't sure he was recovered enough to immediately put himself through something so debilitating that he might be left unconscious on the icy floor.

"I was just thinking--" Bru started.

"You mean you do that?" Draugra's type could not resist sneering at an unfortunate.

"--that the gap between our two intelligences is greater than I originally thought now that I give it more consideration."

The plainsman continued speaking as though uninterrupted.

"Aside from the vast amount of information that you forced upon me," he said, "my mind also contains the intelligences and memories of two uniquely different men from different worlds and backgrounds--while your mind holds but the one set of memories; and not even a millionth of the data that I possess."

Draugra grimaced. "Do not tempt me to demonstrate the capabilities of the devices attached to your body, Troggy old boy. They allow me to send impulses which are translated into a pain response in the wearer."

"My name is Bru--not Troggy."

"And your *title* is assistant," the other stressed. "You would do well to remember it. You shall assist me in repairing my ship so I can leave this Lyra-forsaken place before this volcano erupts and blows the top off of this mountain and incinerates everything within a hundred *phmiles* of here."

4

11. The Plasma Folder

In Bru's dizzy mind spun a phantasmagoria of imagery of all the various types of vessels with which Draugra was familiar as the hunter followed vision after vision of sailing across the skies and piercing the wondrous, colorful cloudscape of the Xylan's world, and many others. Through the medium of Draugra's memories Bru sped over exotic lands, zipped between immense voids of space and picnicked on the dark sides of moons--occasionally accompanied by the radiant Penelephii.

Although he would never admit it to Draugra, he found it fascinating to sift through the other man's memories--a duplicate of which were now his--allowing him to vicariously experience all manner of things of which Bru, the simple hunter, never dreamed. The oddest sensation of the whole, bizarre experience was, for him, pondering the utter starkness of their contrasting lives--his own, lived as one bound to the earth who stared into the sky with wonder, while Draugra was given his first flyer as a child.

Bru learned in an instant--insofar as flyers were concerned--that nothing could compare to seeing the real deal. Memories were one thing; but when he first laid eyes on Draugra's ship his heart initially hammered in his chest with the age-old instinctive fear of the unknown that had been Bru, the hunter's, when faced with the unfamiliar. But the next instant his heart pounded with excitement--the ship was magnificent!

Exiting the icy chamber via a vent shaft that led into the mountain's interior where the hunter had spent his last several weeks, they emerged under the sky which Bru had begun to doubt he would ever again see. Here, the primitive savage was astonished to find a streamlined craft sitting on a broad shelf below the rim of the volcano's crater.

Bru saw in the ship a thing of refined intelligence and beauty that caused him to feel a measure of grudging respect for the race that could build such a thing; it was the epitome of elegance--inspiring, and sleek. His new command of language came to his immense satisfaction now in applying the appropriate terminology to describe the wonder of this futuristic vessel from another world.

As to its *philot?* The newly-learned epithets which Bru mentally applied to his Xylan torturer would have enraged the other had he known; Bru made sure he did not. Following their initial arguments after Bru miraculously survived the tutoring sessions--which the plainsman referred to as torturing sessions--they mutually agreed to refrain from further name calling although Bru still caught the other on the cusp of calling him "Troggy" (insinuating that Bru was a troglodyte, a charge Bru firmly denied since his people had never dwelled in caves) or, "Useful *phidiot*" on occasion.

Draugra eventually became more adept at stifling his insulting impulses which Bru came to believe stemmed from the man's arrogant pride of race and bad habit more so than from an actual feeling of intellectual superiority regarding Bru's intelligence which--the Xylan would have been forced to admit--was greater than the Xylan's own. Yet that leading consonant always gave away the Xylan's inclination to do so, and always caused Bru to grimace and stew in silent rage.

The vessel upon which he was forced to slave was a Xylan *Z2 Plasma Folder,* thus named for its method of folding minute sections of space a light-year or so in dimension. From his forced-memories, Bru was aware of the differences of operation between this type of system as opposed to the later *Mine Borer* technology, so-called after the similarity in operation to a machine used to bore tunnels.

A *Mine Borer* craft fashioned its own worm hole before it and closed it after. The distinction between the two was, Bru reflected, much the same as comparing an old ram jet of the early, Xylan jet age to a later, solid fueled rocket; a *Plasma Folder* got the job done but was less capable; however, it was still effective in its own right and had the added benefit of being cheaper to operate whereas a single trip in a *Borer* craft would bankrupt most.

As the hunter's eyes ran down the sleek lines of the ship the purpose of every component leaped to mind as his newly engrained knowledge identified these features with casual ease even though this was his first time physically laying eyes on them. The damage 4 to the vessel was extensive along the port side. What made it worse was that the damage had gotten into plasma nozzles twelve through fifteen. These were advanced engineering marvels that would not be easy to repair.

Draugra watched Bru's eyes carefully as the hunter took-in the ship for the first time. "I see recognition in your expression; that's good. The knowledge transfer seems to have been successful in that regard. Do you understand the extent of the damage, then? I wish to gauge your assessment, obviously."

"Certainly, I do," the reply came without hesitation. "The *Phroxan Phibre* skin of the vessel from amidships to stern along the port side has been punctured in multiple locations; those damaged tiles will have to be replaced. Plasma nozzles twelve thru fifteen will have to be rebuilt almost from scratch; that's unfortunate. The frames might be salvageable, together with the dark matter parsers but we won't know until they've been removed and disassembled. Oh, and the *Stakk-O-Lan* tubing on the port-side rear landing strut appears to have a slight puncture."

"Say what?" Draugra looked hard at the strut Bru indicated and saw that that the ship had indeed begun to settle ever-so-slightly on that corner. The difference in height between that and the starboard strut could have been no more than the thickness of a dozen hairs. "Ah. I see. You are correct."

"Continuing," Bru said, "had you followed protocol, none of this damage would have occurred."

"What did you just say?"

To Bru's mind the other spoke rather abruptly, and his words came out way too fast one after the other, which only further cemented his suspicions.

"You wanted to land in this crater so that the ship would be hidden from locals like the hillmen; I can understand why that would be desirable. But you obviously turned off the shielding prior to shutting off the atmospheric engines, which is against protocol. On top of precipitately killing the shielding, you landed too close to the crater wall where the port-side nozzles triggered the rock fall that damaged your vessel; scorch marks are still visible on the remaining rock. If you'd landed closer to the edge of the shelf and further from the cliff, this would not have happened. Had you left your shielding up until you shut down the engines this would not have happened. The state in which you find yourself, then, is of your own making."

Draugra's face had perceptibly darkened during Bru's condemnation. "Is that all?"

Bru faced the other man with squared shoulders and an unflinching gaze. "No, I have one further assessment. You landed too close to the crater wall because you were terrified of the ship slipping over the rim should you have risked landing closer to the edge. The resulting damage is, therefore, a product of your being a coward!"

12. Mining for Minerals

With the attachments on his body preventing him from approaching Draugra any closer than two paces or going any further distant than a Xylan *phmile*, Bru found he had no other choice but to help his captor in whatever capacity was required of him to repair the ship as expeditiously as possible so that he might eventually gain his freedom. In return, Draugra promised that he would release the plainsman from bondage, remove the devices from his body and allow him to return to his people after the repairs were complete.

"While I begin removal of the plasma nozzles, I wish you to prospect for a viable substitute to replace the hull paneling and a material to replenish the fuel cells."

"Me? I am a plainsman. I don't care for the mountain heights in which you decided to wreck your ship. It would be best if I disassembled the nozzles while *you* descend into the mountain's interior to prospect for whatever it is you require."

As well argue with solid stone, Bru philosophized later as he was descending a frightful abyss. He was helpless. If he could, he would have wrapped his powerful fingers about the man's throat and snapped his neck, pressing his thumbs into the flesh until they reached the man's worthless spine. As it was, the hunter was forced to mine ores deep in the recesses of the mountain's innards for the necessary elements to make repairs and energize the fuel cells.

The elements used to manufacture the tough *Phroxan Phibre* did not exist on Bru's world but given the scientific knowledge that was now his, and tools aboard the ship that were at his disposal, he was able to determine substitutes that would get the job done.

It was in quest of these minerals that he spent many weeks in dark recesses over horrendous falls above magma calderas and ice caves. With his old fears of mountain heights haunting him, Bru found he must swallow his horror along with his saliva and continue prospecting, being careful not to stray too far lest he be shocked by Draugra's devices and--being rendered senseless--fall to his death.

Being always careful not to approach too close to his captor for fear of being rendered unconscious or outright slain, Bru utilized equipment found aboard the ship to fabricate the panels needing replacement. It was fortunate for Draugra that he had elected to obtain an older scientific vessel and not a mere pleasure vessel which would not have possessed such an elaborate facility which enabled Bru to perform analyses and manufacture materials.

Having discovered an uncharted planet and becoming stranded on it, no one would ever come seeking Draugra here. Had he chosen a simple transit vessel, he could have lived out his life on this planet, a castaway, unable to repair the one thing that could take him home. But it made sense to Bru why Draugra would have chosen such a craft, given that he was a man of science on his own world. Naturally he would desire a ship with full research capability.

This vessel, a Xylan Z2, came standard equipped with a laboratory and machine shop in which every part of the ship might be reproduced as long as the raw materials to do so could be obtained. And there were practicable substitutes for most of these materials that were to be found on every world--the basic building blocks of stars and planets. The one thing the ship did lack, though, was a full contingent of crew capable of utilizing the impressive array of equipment; where the vessel should have held a compliment of a dozen crewmen Draugra had chosen to venture on his ill-fated expedition alone.

Less Draugra wax arrogant and brag of the exotic materials that were available on his homeworld but were not to be found on Bru's world, the hunter pointed out certain elements he discovered in the bowels of the mountain which were superior to the comparable material on Xyla. One of these--a pure, yellow metal--Bru sat testing at a metering station for its electrical conducting properties when Draugra approached.

Pausing at the minimum distance to avoid discharging the devices installed on Bru's body, Draugra commented on the material that the other was testing.

"Naturally it cannot hope to transfer vibrating atoms as smoothly or with the rapidity of Xylan *phrobon*, but perhaps it will suffice until I return home and can have the connections replaced," the Xylan said. His tone literally dripped arrogant derision.

Bru finished plasma-soldering a connection, switched the settings on his meter and grunted in satisfaction as he scanned the reading, sounding much like the old Bru as he did so--the Bru who had no idea what an electron was. "This material is actually a far better conductor than your *phrobon* ever thought about being. Look for yourself."

Bru stepped away from the test equipment so that Draugra could take a look; now it was the Xylan who grunted--only not in self-satisfaction. Draugra suddenly found he had nothing further to say on the matter and, doing an about face, he stalked off.

Bru manufactured hundreds of the small *phibre* panels and then he and Draugra worked laboriously to install them, Bru being careful to always maintain several paces distance to the Xylan. While the plainsman was fabricating these panels, the *philot* was disassembling the damaged plasma nozzles. Of them, three would require the fabrication of new dark matter parsers and all four required new housings.

It was the repair of these plasma nozzles for which Draugra had been in particular need of an assistant. They required calibration which dictated that one person be at the nozzle while another sat at the controls in the cabin. Before this, Bru had already been introduced to the standard Xylan headset with their built-in wireless communicators. Wearing a protective suit to prevent his being injured during the calibration, he and Draugra, in close communication, worked through the cumbersome process, step by tedious step.

Regarding the volcano, Bru only learned of its existence when Draugra explained that an eruption was imminent. It had never erupted during his peoples' lifetimes so Bru--the Bru who knew nothing of spacecraft and helmet-educators--had been completely oblivious of their existence. Draugra said that it was his opinion that this one had been inactive for millennia.

So, in addition to laboriously gathering materials and making repairs, Draugra also set Bru to monitoring the volcano sensors he installed when he arrived two years before. The hunter now understood that, although the evidence was completely undetectable to the naked eye, an eruption did indeed loom. The readings on certain of Draugra's sensors were irrefutable. And it was these readings that interested Bru above all else since the safety of his people was at stake should the mountain decide to blow. While he was cleaning a dark matter parser, he kept glancing at one of the seismographic meters.

"The meter for location C2 keeps spiking," he commented. "That's on the south-west slope, close to the lake above the encampment of my people."

"Yes, I'm aware; it's my belief that is where the caldera below the planet crust will break through to the surface. The readings cause me to feel the main vent shaft has become partially blocked and it has found an additional outlet. It will not be good to be within two degrees of latitude of this range when it blows; it's going to take the entire range with it."

"It would take at least a week to move my people that distance. We are nearly finished here. When can I leave?"

"After we're finished."

But Bru noticed that Draugra turned his face away when he replied and that he averted his eyes. It was at this moment that the hunter thought that perhaps psychology had its uses, after all.

"You are certain?" he pressed.

Draugra looked at him oddly. "Yes, I agree, we are nearly finished here."

13. Folding Space

Bru awakened to the sensation of a palpable vibration beneath him. He lay asleep in one of the comfortably heated cabins aboard the vessel--a room given over to his use by Draugra after they began repair work on the ship. Given the frigid temperatures on the peaks of the snowcapped mountain range, the hunter was glad. He might have bundled up and survived the frigid clime of the mountain heights but was glad he did not have to.

The vibrations he was experiencing he initially assumed to be Draugra testing the ship's engines earlier than planned; they were supposed to test later that day. Bru snapped wide awake--after the testing, he was to be freed! It was then that he discerned that the vibrations did not come from the vessel but rather were being passed to the vessel from the mountain beneath it; Draugra rapped on the cabin door.

"Open," Bru hissed. At his voice-command, the door slid aside.

"We just experienced a slight tremor," the Xylan announced. "It wasn't severe, but severe enough to cause me to advance liftoff. I ran the diagnostics again; it passed all tests twice at one-hundred *phercent*; I deem the craft to be space-worthy. But if we sit here idly for much longer the ship may be incinerated together with both of us before we could finish a single nozzle test."

Bru leaped to his feet at the first mention of the volcano. "*We* are not going to sit idly here or anywhere. You do not need me for the nozzle testing or lifting off or anything else. Even if something small needed repaired, at this point you're capable of doing so yourself. The bulk of the work has been done by me. I demand that you release me so I can return to my people and get them to a place of safety away from this mountain!"

Draugra's eyes narrowed. The man's lips were gravened in a thin, tight line across his inflexible features. "I told you that you would be my assistant for as long as I deemed necessary. You may not realize it, but you are a medical miracle. You're going to make me famous, Bru--and wealthy, I've no doubt. No one has ever successfully transmitted as much data as I did to you. I killed half a tribe of mountain men before I was successful; but it was worth every single one of their filthy, rotting, stinking hides! Just wait until they see you on Xyla."

While he was still speaking Draugra stepped within the confines of the sleeping chamber, effectively blocking Bru's escape. The hunter could not shove his way past the other without causing the devices attached to his body to activate, rendering him unconscious. Draugra continued to approach the hunter.

"Stay back!" Bru warned.

"I knew you would be disagreeable to this change of plan." Draugra continued his slow pace across the cabin floor. "I cannot wait for Penelephii to see you. She's a fellow biologist--but you know that! So you also know how excited she will be to learn of your world and its inherent possibilities. Not only have I intelligenced a savage with the knowledge of millions of scientists, but I have discovered a new world; one unexplored by our people-- we who would explore the deepest reaches of space!"

"No, you can't! Draugra--"

The Xylan rushed him. Bru felt the bite of ten-thousand stingers as the devices he wore poured relentless, debilitating voltage into his body. He was barely able to remain standing when Draugra grasped him by his upper arms, the Xylan somehow insulated from the current coursing through his victim; and then Bru felt himself falling.

"Stubborn *phebiistart*," he heard the other man mutter.

***

When Bru awakened it was to a sound with which he was quite familiar even though this was the first time he'd heard it with his own ears. It was the hum of plasma nozzles doing what plasma nozzles do best--relentlessly folding light-years of space and releasing pent energy.

The hunter rose and looked out a port hole. His chamber was on the port side; outside lay a black starfield and while he looked there appeared the most beautiful planet he'd ever seen. In point of fact, it was the only planet he had ever seen from space; but this didn't matter because he was unconsciously comparing it to the images stored in his memories, and these were as real to him as if they were his own.

Xyla was stunning, there was no denying it. It was marbled with seas and lakes and continents. Unlike Bru's world, Xyla's oceans and land masses were divided nearly equally. As a result, instead of the blue given off by the hunter's mostly-water covered world, this planet emitted a soft palette of blues and greens and yellows and sapphires and other colors of a different spectrum which, due to his inculcated memories, felt natural to him.

He heard a sound in his earpiece; it was Draugra.

"We're here."

"I know where we are, you *phidiot*," Bru whispered for his own benefit. Finding he could stand steadily, he ordered the door, "Open!" The door remained steadfast in its sealed position.

"I couldn't have you running about the ship while I was flying, Troggy old boy."

In his mind, Bru could see the Xylan's lip curling in haughty scorn. A thousand sharp retorts rose to Bru's lips; but after careful consideration, he bit each one back. He had hunted Kusk the bear and Pooph the giant sloth; he had lain quietly in wait for Ros the Elk, and other, mightier beasts; together with the other hunters of the tribe he had stalked Moosh the Mammoth. Now Draugra had added his name to the list of beasts that Bru, hunter of the Tribe of the Seven Rivers, would with the infinite patience of the wild, hunt and harvest, no matter how long it took him.

14. A New Agreement

Bru gazed listlessly out a port hole as clouds drifted soundlessly past. Leveling off after a rapid descent from space, they were currently shooting through a softly glowing Xylan sky. The radiant pinks and oranges, however, did nothing to make Bru's mood any rosier.

The cabin door slid aside at Draugra's command, having placed the ship on *phautomatic*. Bru didn't bother turning to face the Xylan. He would bide his time until he could take the man's head. It wouldn't be the head of Tysk that he had longed to harvest all those months ago--but right now it was the head he wished for the most.

"There is something we need to clear up before we land."

Bru continued to gaze out the window, watching as they dropped below the cloud cover and continued their descent over a mountain range. Beyond this range, he saw that the land plunged in elevation to lush green forests and hills.

"I already know what you're going to say, so you may as well save your breath."

"Oh? And what is that?" Draugra crossed his arms as though interested in what the other might say.

"You've come to warn me against telling my own version of why I'm here or that you're a spineless worm and a real piece of bear scat."

Bru turned from the view port to face the cabin. The sight of the vertical mountain slopes caused his heart to lurch, but no longer with the unnerving fear of the past. Having lived in their shadow his entire life, they now--after hovering on the precipice of the firmament and gazing upon the surface of a world--only served to remind him so strongly of home that he could scarcely stand it.

"You're a bigger coward than I initially estimated," he continued. "I've been thinking--perhaps I was doing so the entire time I was unconscious which was due to yet another of your cowardly acts. I've deduced some things about the time you spent on my world; about the time we spent repairing this vessel--about

5

everything leading up to this moment where I shall soon find myself enslaved on a strange world."

"You are hardly a slave. Well, not in the strictest sense of the word, at least," Draugra replied. "At least you won't have to labor as do some. Whatever you think of me you'd best keep to yourself. If you're good, I'll return you to your native world . . . eventually. Honestly, it might not be in time to save your hunter-gathering friends--I really couldn't say. But something's better than nothing, right? The council will wish to take readings. It isn't like you'll be locked in a cage and studied like an animal--not that you aren't one."

Bru kept any further comments to himself but inwardly he was fuming. During the calibration of the plasma nozzles Draugra was sitting at the flight controls, switching between them; Moosh could have been trained to do so if he could have squeezed into the *philot's* chair. The entire thing could have been done remotely, for that matter, by a single person; Bru presence hadn't really been necessary. It had all been contrived to keep the plainsman cooperative until Draugra deemed it was time to leave, since the Xylan could have accomplished the calibration by himself, in Bru's opinion.

Bru had performed all of the more technical repairs to the ship, from gathering raw material to processing atoms, to manufacturing required molecules. The Xylan once mentioned that many hillmen perished while undergoing the treatment to create someone who was intelligent enough to assist in repairing the ship, treatments which Bru felt he had only barely survived himself. He felt that Draugra perpetrated his wanton acts of cruelty on one ignorant native after another until he found one who could survive. But to what end?

"So," Draugra was saying, "after they perform their tests and are satisfied that my claims are valid, I can arrange to have you returned home. "

Home. The word caused Bru to think of Oona. Thoughts of the girl caused his hand to involuntarily reach for the necklace he carved for her so long ago out of the piece of tough, rhinoceros' horn, and which she gifted him back to remember her by when he was cast out of the tribe by her father. The necklace!

"Where is my necklace? You said when we finished repairs of the ship I could have it back. Where is it?" Bru felt his heart racing, pounding in his chest like the thunderous pads of some stampeding herd.

Draugra looked genuinely confused for a moment, causing Bru's heart to sink. "Necklace? Oh! Well . . ." he hedged. "I forgot it in the cavern--it was in that *pthellow*-colored storage chest which was left behind. No matter! I'll return you to your tribe shortly and you can make another one. And while you do so, you can tell your hairy friends of your adventures on another planet--not that they'll believe you. Actually, in their primitive, barbaric tongue, you probably won't be able to go into much detail, will you?"

Draugra seemed to find some thought he had humorous because he began smiling. "I have it! Tell them that I was a sorcerer! A sorcerer who took you to another world! I've been mistaken for such before by primates, it's quite amusing really. Your people have sorcerers, right? Witch doctors? Shamans? I'm sure that you do! This could be to your advantage. You just have to put the right spin on it. Threaten them that if they do not do your bidding, your friend the sorcerer shall return and blast them with his fires!"

"They've probably already been blasted with fire, you *pthakking phidiot*!"

Bru squeezed his fists until his palms bled, a habit of his when he was really angry and trying not to show it. Then a thought of the necklace gifted him from sweet Oona being blasted in the eruption, in effigy of the fate doomed to overtake his people--including the one whom he held most dear--brought forth a torrent of tears; the tears of one who is completely and utterly heartbroken and despondent. When he spoke next, the pain he was suffering caused his voice to take on a perceptible edge.

"You could have allowed me to warn them. I could have saved them. But you had to flee--like the coward you are. You're always acting the coward! I won't tell the council about you, Draugra. Not

6

unless I begin the story with, 'I'm going to tell you about the greatest coward I ever met!'"

"You dare!" Draugra took a step closer and Bru felt the tingling in the devices begin.

"Come on!" His roar caused the veins in his temples to throb. He took a step toward the other in pure defiance. "Zap me with your stupid electric devices! Is that what makes you feel like a big man? Does utilizing your technological torture devices against the disadvantaged make you feel somehow taller, Draugra? You *phebiistart*! You and your vaunted intelligence. Don't forget--*sorcerer*-- that I'm smarter than you by thousands fold. I could design this ship from the ground up, but you--you're barely smart enough to push its buttons!"

15. Penelephii

Bru, formerly a hunter of the Tribe of the Seven Rivers, and the sorcerous Draugra, a scientist and explorer from another world, glared at one another with wrath-filled eyes that emanated palpable and mutual hatred and dislike.

"You should know that there is little speaking requirement for the testing you shall undergo, so you better calm the *pthak* down or I'll remove your vocal chords prior to landing and tell my conferees that you shouted until I was forced to take those measures."

"You would," Bru spat. "My anger is justified, and you know it. Yet still it rates a cowardly lie from your foul lips. No surprise there! Never fear, Draugra. I'll leave it to you to reveal your creation to the world. By Lyra--now you've got me swearing by your *pthakking* goddess--I can't comprehend how they've not seen through your shallow facade by now. Or maybe they have and you're a laughingstock and don't even know it."

Draugra issued the, "Close!" command to shut the door behind him more loudly than necessary when he stormed from Bru's cabin to return forward to the control room.

Bru, petrified of what might be happening on his homeworld at that very instant, became more and more livid with each passing moment as that was the only sentiment that approached anywhere close to giving him relief from his pent emotion. The thought of Oona being vaporized by a volcano filled him with crawling horror while the irreverence Draugra displayed in leaving the necklace Bru had carved for the girl to be destroyed made his temples pound with rage. He leaped to his feet and paced the short distance between the walls of his confines.

It wasn't losing a bit of horn that he had harvested at great risk in his daring youth that caused its loss to affect him so. The carving had come to signify his growing affection for the girl and stood as a reminder to a relationship that in the end had been all too brief and bittersweet. He knew he could never be with her now for she had long since been mated to Gla. Also, the chances were great that she would be dead before he could ever hope to rescue her. Thus, out

6

of all his possessions, this memento meant more to him than his own life.

On a whim, he looked at his cabin door and said, "Open." His eyebrows raised a tad when it *whooshed* aside.

He was as familiar with the narrow confines of the curving halls of the science vessel as was Draugra and so wasted no time making his way forward. That door, also, slid aside at his command. He took a seat in a navigation officer's chair a couple of paces from the Xylan without a word.

"I thought you might prefer a change of scenery. Although one can look out the portholes in the cabins, the forward viewscreen offers a wider panorama. Beautiful, isn't it? I've always enjoyed this particular stretch of topography, sailing from the mountains into the lowlands below the lake."

Bru stared. The mountains--which were behind them by now--lay north of this beautiful, serene lake. Reflected in its still surface were skies of incredible pastels. Lush grassland stretched toward far away, distant hills. Bru's heart pounded in his chest. The vista reminded him much of the plains back home whereon camped his people.

Rearing far above the hills ahead of them, however, was a sight not to be found on his homeworld--the buildings of a glittering and towering city. He could see the distant mountains, the lake, the rolling grasslands, the sky--all of it was reflected in the mirror-like surfaces of the looming structures which were so many in number and built so close upon one another that the reflected image appeared like an immense tapestry suspended before them. Draugra caused the ship to make for one of the *phmiles*-high towers, eventually settling upon a landing pad protruding on a certain level.

The pair wasted little time exiting the vessel. For Bru, who'd been unconscious until only recently, the trip did not seem to have been of long duration--making him wonder if Draugra had maintained him in a state of oblivion by some unknown means. However that may be, Bru was not accustomed to such confines for any length of time and wanted out; he desired to feel air moving across his body and to see the sky over his head. He knew, however, that his time out-of-doors would be short lived. There were the scans to make--three dimensional biological views showing the effects of the helmet-educator devices on the brain of a lower order; such things always interested the Xylans.

As they walked across the landing platform toward the entrance it slid open before they could reach it and a woman stepped outside to meet them--a woman the sight of whom caused Bru's heart to race. For he recognized her in an instant; it was Penelephii, one whom the confusing memories of her lovemaking teased throughout his brain in the intermingled memories of he and the despicable, self-proclaimed "sorcerer" who walked beside him whose pathetic memories had not done the girl one bit of justice.

"Draugra? Is it really you?"

The girl, tall and curvier than a mountain path, approached Draugra and hugged him. She did not press herself into him, Bru noticed, as one might expect of a pining lover. When a man of Bru's tribe returned from afield his woman rushed to him and grasped him so tightly that a hand could not be inserted between them; for, when a hunter left of a morn there existed the very real chance that he might not return. Bru noticed a sliver of light between the tips of the girl's breasts and Draugra's torso that caused him to wonder.

Penelephii stepped back quickly and cast a disarming smile at Draugra.

"Penelephii! You--" the sorcerer started.

The entry *swooshed* again to permit the passage of another--a man this time. "Ah, Draugra, old boy! You've returned! Quite the expedition, that!"

Draugra snapped his mouth shut without finishing what he had started to say. "Pylapharum. Yes, it was quite an expedition." Draugra's focus shot back to Penelephii. "I was going to say, Penelephii, that you would not believe how I have missed you. You cannot know what it is like to be stranded on an uncharted planet for two years. But it was worth it! You will see."

The girl smiled on one side of her mouth, but Bru noticed that it did not quite reach her eyes. "Two years? Has it really been that long?"

"Yes," Draugra said a trifle coolly, "at least it was for some of us."

"We wondered where you ran off to," the girl smoothed. "You said you would be gone for . . . what was it--a couple of weeks, wasn't it?"

"When you failed to return after four months," Pylapharum informed, "I cued the authorities to be on the lookout for your ship's signal. They never detected one; at least so far as I know. You must have been some where quite distant, eh Draugra?"

The sorcerer glowered at Pylapharum. "Four months? You waited that long before informing the authorities I was missing? I might have died, waiting for rescuers! Luckily, I was resourceful, as you shall both see. Come, Bru."

"Uncharted planet did you say?" Pylapharum asked. This idea seemed to perk his interest, even if Draugra's return did not.

"Now, Draugra," purred Penelephii.

Bru stared. What man could resist those lips, that dimple, that dipping décolletage or the sparkles in those insanely riveting, green eyes? The hunter shook his head. Wait--were those his own thoughts just now? Or Draugra's? It was all so confusing--Draugra's memories of the girl were suddenly coming alive while in her presence like they never had on Bru's world. Now the sorcerer's memories were threatening to supplant his own thoughts and feelings for Oona. Forcefully, he tore his eyes away from the girl's magnificent form and found something interesting on the floor to stare at.

"Don't be distraught, dear," she continued, still speaking to Draugra. "You told us you might be away for longer than that, remember? Now, who is this . . . Bru, was it? What a singular, monosyllabic name!"

Bru looked up to find her inquisitive gaze upon him. That dimple again. The hunter could remain silent no longer.

"I am Bru." He stepped just slightly ahead of Draugra, being mindful to maintain his distance to the sorcerer; it wouldn't do to be shocked into a lather and collapse to one's knees before this raven-haired goddess--that would be mortifying. With the memories of proper etiquette and the manners by which one must comport oneself in society coursing through his head at least half as intoxicatingly as was his blood in his veins, he bent over the girl's hand.

Although he was not as tall as Draugra--whose great height caused him to appear a bit gaunt, in Bru's opinion--yet Bru was still taller than the girl who must perforce look up to meet his steadfast gaze. Bru was built like the statue of a god in some Xylan city that didn't worship bare-breasted Lyra, causing the girl's eyes in turn to roam involuntarily over his hard frame as though they had a mind of their own and she was just along for the ride; Bru swore he could hear the sorcerer grind his teeth.

"Bru, of the Seven Rivers tribe of plainsmen. And you are Penelephii. Although we've never met, I recall a certain night on Pylon's outer moon as if it were but yesterday," he blurted before he could stop himself.

16. On Xyla

Bru realized an instant after he spoke that he was not supposed to know of that particular encounter, and that the girl--who was now taking a hard look at Draugra--might not appreciate having the occasion mentioned in so casual a manner in mixed company. He next recalled that the sorcerer did not wish any mention of the educator-helms; such a memory could only be explained by their use. This was to be Draugra's revelation, to divulge in a manner that would gain him notoriety, the accomplishment of which was supposed to gain Bru his freedom.

"You shall have to overlook anything he says, Penelephii. The inhabitants of his world have yet to develop a *Phidula Phortex*; he says whatever pops into his little hunter-gatherer mind."

"I've brought down Kusk the bear within two paces of me," Bru assured Draugra--who was standing roughly two paces distant.

"He doesn't look like the gatherer type to me; hunter . . . sure," Penelephii breathed. Her mouth curved into a smile that she could not have prevented had she wished to.

Bru dragged his eyes from hers to find Draugra staring fixedly at him, silently daring the savage to say another word. Bru couldn't argue against the sorcerer's accusation about the development of his brain, however. It was true that his people were accustomed to speaking their minds. Since Draugra spoke a simple fact in this instance, Bru chose to remain quiet--but it was for that reason alone that he refrained from further comment; he held no physical fear of the sorcerer, only the dread that the man might prevent him from ultimately returning home, which was his only and greatest fear.

The girl did not appear to be cross from Bru's frank outburst, which in turn caused the hunter to find it odd that he didn't wish to offend her and was thereby relieved when she did not seem angry with him. Instead it was to Draugra that she returned her attention. Bru hoped she would rip into him soundly for the hunter's reference to Pylon's moon and braced to make every attempt to *not* stifle the grin that such a thrashing was sure to produce on his handsome features.

"Pylon's outer moon? I've only been there once or twice, Draugra--when you and I were seeing each other for a few months, as I recall. Bru's mention of it causes me to wonder how he knows of this. Surely you didn't tell your friend tales about us?"

"No, no of course not; maybe I mentioned it in passing," the sorcerer of Xyla dissembled, sheepishly. "And he's not my friend, Penelephii--he's an accomplishment. Just . . . forget it for the time being, would you? We can discuss all of this later when I shall explain everything. I believe you will be quite astounded when you hear what I have to say!"

"Alright, Draugra. Since you landed here at the council center, I assume I would not find you in your apartments later tonight, then?"

The insinuation that she was familiar with the sorcerer's apartments, in combination with the smile the girl was suddenly wearing, caused Bru's heart to begin pounding violently in his chest again. He could only imagine what Draugra might be experiencing if the effect of the sorcerer's embedded memories in the hunter's brain were any indication.

The girl was certainly confounding. She had at first appeared to have little interest in the sorcerer and now here she was, nonchalantly offering to visit him in his rooms.

That last thought caused memories to flood Bru's mind of his own sweet Oona visiting him secretly in his shelter the night before he was exiled from the tribe. The recollection brought with it a flood of shame as he recalled the rapid beating of his heart caused by Penelephii's seductive smile just now. He was beginning to find it impossible to separate his own feelings from those implanted by Draugra!

"Ah, um, that is, no," stumbled Draugra. "I haven't set foot in my quarters for over two years, so a few more days will make little difference. We shall billet here in the guest chambers tonight. I must see the council first thing."

The girl was difficult to read. Did she seem . . . pleased? Disappointed? Intrigued? Bru could not say with certainty.

6

"Then the two of you should join us in the morning," she replied smoothly. "We shall break our *phast* together, and you may tell us more about Bru, perhaps--and exactly what it is you have supposedly accomplished."

By the time she finished speaking she was no longer looking at Draugra although her comments had been directed at him. Rather, her eyes slid sideways mid-reply so that by the time her tongue graced her last sentence with a period she was looking at the plainsman.

Ignoring the confused looks from his peers, Draugra ushered Bru towards the doorway that provided ingress into the complex.

Raising his eyebrows and cocking his head askance at Penelephii, Pylapharum steered the girl ahead of him with a slight touch of his hand upon the small of her back--a touch that Draugra, although he was leading the way, did not fail to notice.

Bru did not fail to notice it either, although it did not make him jealous. Instead, he smiled because he knew it would incense Draugra. But a moment later he frowned as his own thoughts alternated between memories of Penelephii--and Oona.

***

The next morning Draugra came to summon Bru. Given the earliness of the hour, the sorcerer expected to have the pleasure of rousing the plainsman from his bed; but in this he was disappointed. Bru had awakened a full two hours prior to Draugra's entering his chamber. Aggravated--and not a little alarmed--the Xylan sped from the hunter's chambers and sought his charge amongst the various halls of the council level.

The man was alarmed because, at Bru's request prior to retiring the previous evening, Draugra relented and removed the control devices from the other's body. The sorcerer had been inclined to leave them in place to assert his dominion over the other but was reminded that, given that hundreds of light-years lay between their worlds and that there existed zero chance that the hunter could escape, that they were no longer necessary. The most convincing factor was that they were becoming an increasing nuisance to both men due to their proximity since leaving Bru's primitive world.

By this time Bru had already broken his fast with an inquisitive Pylapharum and Penelephii with whom he became better acquainted during the course of their meal. Then, accompanied by Draugra's two conferees he'd taken a stroll out of doors on a walkway so high above the surface that the details below were fuzzy with vapor and distance. The simple plainsman found it awe inspiring and not a little frightening to gaze--not up--but down, upon clouds.

Although they plied Bru with questions, both direct and subtle, yet was the hunter careful not to mention anything that would give Draugra further cause to become incensed and spiteful with him. There was still the barest chance that the sorcerer might keep his word, have his moment of glory--which was to bring the Xylan wealth and acclaim--and then return the savage to his homeworld in time to effect the tribe's escape from the volcanic eruption. Sifting through the massive amount of knowledge stored in his head alongside the memories of two men, he knew stranger things had happened.

As the trio entered the biology annex, they were laughing at a story Bru was relating of his accidentally entering the den of a cave bear to do his business while on a hunting expedition. A bear--whom, unbeknownst to him, was inside asleep at the time--awakened while Bru's mammoth's-hide breeches were down around his ankles.

"So, there I was, my breeks down to my feet, trying to run, falling down every other step with an angry, half-asleep cave bear as big as a flyer ambling sleepily along behind me, grunting as it caught my scent--which was quite potent at that particular moment. I'd left my spear leaning against a wall of the cave in my rush to escape, for Lyra's sakes, and was hopping along trying to simultaneously pull up my breeks and not end up face down in the dirt with Kusk taking a bite out of my backside."

Penelephii beamed. "Oh, my! But that sounds adventurous! We have no such things here as these Kusks you speak of! Are they very large?"

Those eyes; those dimples! Bru tried to push the thoughts away but found it difficult when she was in such close proximity and smelled so sweetly of blooming *philacs*.

"Oh, they're humungous. One of them could pull Draugra apart like a wishbone and use one of his *phemurs* to *phloss* its teeth. Yes, they're big, nasty brutes, all right."

Pylapharum, waiting for a pause in the conversation, interjected, "Well, don't keep us in suspense, Bru! Were you able to escape?"

Bru laughed and Penelephii tittered intoxicatingly.

"Well, I mean--" began Pylapharum, embarrassed. "Obviously, you did; I suppose I meant, how--"

"You're right, Pylapharum," spat Draugra nastily. The sorcerer, looking as sour as he sounded, approached the three from a blind side. "It *is* obvious. Bru, if you would; I have arranged a meeting with the council in fifteen *tarts*."

Glancing at Penelephii, Draugra added with less edge to his tone, "Upon my request they acceded to the presence of you and Pylapharum, as well."

"Of course," she replied; all business now, dimples fading. "We shall see you in a few *tarts*, then." She looked at Bru and her grin returned, obviously still tickled from the hunter's story. "Bye, Bru. See you in a bit."

Following Draugra, Bru knew what awaited him. The instant they were alone the sorcerer would turn on him and blast him for his temerity and lack of judgement in sneaking out before Draugra awakened and for speaking without permission with the sorcerer's contemporaries. He was surprised, however, when the man said not a word about any of that as they entered a section of deserted hallway. Instead, he railed against Pylapharum, his hated rival.

Like Gla.

"I will show them. *Pthakking* Pylapharum! What I have accomplished, the others have never dreamed possible to achieve. To successfully instill intelligence of this magnitude in a lower order--and a non-Xylan! It is a true first."

"You're a regular medicopreneur," Bru commented dryly.

He was tired of being referred to as a "lower" anything. Given the confusing feelings he experienced whenever he was around Penelephii, he counted Draugra's memories as a curse and since his new-found intelligence so far had offered him nothing in the form of a single idea that would return him to his own world, he placed very little value on it.

"I shall become famous, where Pylapharum shall join the dust of the ages and be forgotten. Yes. That is how it shall happen. It is I who shall attain the next seat on the council, whereas he believes he shall be the next to join that dignified body. When I sit on the council, I will send him to Mergodon to study the insect life…"

Draugra's biting threats reminded Bru suddenly and forcefully of the plans he'd had in mind for Gla. To be forced to admit that similarities existed between he and one he found so detestable caused his face to redden.

"That *phebühstahrt*," Draugra continued to rail. "And while he studies bugs on a barren, desert world, Penelephii shall return with me to my new world that I discovered where we shall--"

Draugra stopped in mid-sentence and glanced quickly at his companion. Sensing that the sorcerer had been on the cusp of accidentally admitting something he would rather not say aloud, Bru met his gaze.

"Where you'll what? Why is the fact that you were able to embed this information in my brain so important, Draugra?"

"It's nothing you need bother yourself about, Troggy old boy. Just bear in mind that if all goes well in this council meeting you may very well find yourself enroute to your homeworld--maybe even arriving in time to save your Oona!"

Bru grit his teeth. "I'd better."

Draugra paused before a door and gazed at Bru through narrowed slits. "What you better do is be on your best behavior if you know what's good for you! And here we are."

17. Grilled by the Council

When Bru entered the council chamber it was not into totally unfamiliar surroundings to which he stepped because, although it was the first time that he had passed physically beneath that lintel or lain eyes upon the mind-numbing array of equipment with which the chamber was equipped, it was not the first time he had seen it; for he had entered these hallowed chambers a hundred times in the memories of Draugra.

The council, a body of twenty-two persons, was arcanely arranged so that one never quite faced all of the members simultaneously. The hunter, who preferred to have his back against something solid and for potential enemies to be where he could see them, found it to be slightly disconcerting; certainly, he did not like having them behind him. He began to experience the same sense of heightened alarm as when he had been suddenly surrounded by members of a forest tribe once from whom he only barely escaped. The manner in which they scrambled through the branches like animals still haunted him.

Draugra led Bru to a position in the center of the room which saw the sorcerer seated comfortably behind him while Bru was left standing, exposed for all to see which only furthered the hunter's sense of alarm. The examination platform was in the form of a raised dais which began slowly revolving once they were situated so that Bru eventually, after a full rotation, had faced each of the various members of the council--but never all of them at once.

"Stand there, Bru, and remain still while the scans are made. I told you this would be quick, and so it shall be."

"And harmless?" Bru tensed.

"Yes," the other replied honestly. "The scans are completely harmless."

Like many who live close to the wilds, Bru was an excellent judge of--not only character--but of body language; he saw that the other was being truthful in this instance. Rigid as a statue, he stood where he was told. He only hoped it was over as quickly as was promised. There were untold lightyears of travel ahead of him and he wished to start the journey as soon as possible.

He neither saw nor felt anything, and only looked on as the various members of the council gazed curiously at their *phigitizer*s upon which were being cast the results of the various scans being made of him. The manner in which they leaned-in toward one another--whispering, glancing at the hunter and taking quick glimpses at the sorcerer--caused his brows to furrow in slight aggravation. But no other hint of movement passed through his rigidly poised frame.

"While we await the completion of the tests," the chairman said, "I motion to open the floor for questions and comments. As the council knows, Draugra is on the list of potential candidates being considered for a council appointment when an opening is available. I myself shall open; Draugra, describe for us the reason for your having requested this special session, and explain, if you would, just where in the *Pthell* you've been for the last two years."

"Certainly," Draugra smiled ingratiatingly. "As you are all aware, generations have passed without the advancement of a single new or innovative theory or idea; we have experimented for millennia with knowledge transferal with the hopes of bringing an end to the stagnation of the mind that plagues Xyla. It seems we have already thought every possible thought, and there remains not a solitary, original idea to be discovered. For myself, I blame our laws--"

"I blame the capacity of our craniums," interrupted one. "We max out at ten or so disciplines per lifetime using the educator-helms, having to wait a decade between inducements. To risk going any further is to risk insanity . . . or death."

Bru tensed at that last statement. "What did he just say--"

"Thank you, Councilman Phylbyr--yes, facts of which we are all crystally aware." Draugra's tone was courteous enough, but the expression in his eyes--which bounced between the man to whom he'd replied to, and Bru--was one of vexation. Phylbyr happened to be one of a handful of aging council members whom Draugra wished would just die already and make way for younger members. The appointment to the council was for life, however, and there

7

was no path by which a member might be forced out, much to the frustration of Draugra and others.

"Order, Councilman Phylbyr," concurred the council chair. "You were not recognized and are, therefore, speaking out of order. Continue, Draugra."

Nodding courteously, Draugra picked back up with his tale. "After settling my vessel to the surface of the subject's homeworld, which I discovered by chance and good fortune, an ill-fated rock fall occurred which seriously damaged my vessel. It was as I labored to make repairs that I happened upon the subject one day and rescued him from a number of his fellows who were intent on his life."

Bru slowly turned his head and looked over his shoulder at Draugra.

"Do try to stand still, Bru." The sorcerer smiled at the hunter and continued while Bru bit back any comment.

"Although I found the local inhabitants an intriguing study, the damage my ship suffered was so serious that I'd begun to consider the grave possibility of my never returning to Xyla. You cannot know, incidentally, how the sound of your voices is as music to the hearing bereft who suddenly find their sense restored through one of the miraculous surgeries engineered and performed by the subalterns administered by this honorable council."

"Hear, hear," approved a member, nodding sagely.

"With my vessel smashed beyond my ability to repair it single-handedly was at last generated an idea born of desperation. This poor savage was performing trite, brainless services for me that required only a sturdy back--which he did out of a grateful heart for having saved his life at great risk to my own--while I attempted to make the necessary repairs to my vessel. These repairs demanded the construction of raw materials from the uncharted atoms and molecules of an unknown world; the wonderful minerals of Xyla do not exist there, alas. Lyra, was it tedious!"

"One can well imagine," nodded the chairman. "Your industrious accomplishments regarding the repair of your ship, I must admit, are a surprising revelation and a side of your knowledge inculcation of which we were previously unaware. We hope you were careful when indulging in your increase of information, however, as you obviously found yourself forced to do. There are the unfortunate side effects, as you know. One must take the requisite years in their cranial accumulation."

"Indeed, I am aware of the requisite ten-year hiatus between inculcations," hedged Draugra. "And unfortunately, I was just over mid-way of my staying period. Thus, it was only out of pure necessity that I decided to attempt to inculcate this young savage--"

"What!" exploded Phylbyr.

"--with the necessary Xylan knowledge," Draugra surged forward, raising his voice a trifle to be heard over the gasps of shock from various councilmen and women, "that I might have someone on hand who might assist me in the performance of more complex duties--"

"But . . . knowledge transfer to a non-Xylan--" inserted another.

"--than those" Draugra continued, "which he had previously performed that he might assist me with the task of repairing the engines and exterior panels."

"But the law states--"

"Necessity is a great goad!" burst Draugra at last, exasperated. He knew beforehand that he would have to deal with objections yet had remained unabashed. "I admit," he cajoled, "that besides needing someone technologically gifted to assist with the repairs, there existed the innate Xylan desire to speak with someone of intelligence, even if it was a primordial artificially inseminated with it. This poor fellow's intellect was bordering on that of a single-celled organism. What joy, I thought, could he be made to have thoughts and have an intelligent conversation! And on the subject of conversation, the council, I am sure, can understand where one might become desperate."

"Of a surety," admitted an aged member, "intellect is the atomic building block of the molecular structure known as speech. But still. . . to inculcate a non-Xylan--"

"Certainly, it is," Draugra unctuously agreed with the senior councilman's first statement while studiously ignoring his second. "And toward that goal I brought out the helmet-educators."

Becoming impassioned, Draugra leaped to his feet. He knew by the looks on their faces that no one was buying the hype that his actions were not self-serving but rather a humanitarian outreach to a lower order who might have otherwise been foredoomed to live out its miserable existence in complete and utter ignorance; he no longer cared. As for the restrictions on transferring knowledge to non-Xylans, he would just have to get them to come around to his way of thinking. If he didn't, his gambit would come to naught and he would shortly find himself sitting in an internment chamber.

"Comrades," he smoothed. "I wish you to meet Bru--a former primate savage from an unknown world!"

"Preposterous!" burst Phylbyr. "That man is no more a primate than I am--"

"Ladies and *phentlemen* of the council," inserted Phlibion. "I posit that a great and mighty hoax is being perpetrated upon this council!"

"I wish to pose a question to Draugra." The speaker, having risen, directed her gaze to the council chairman.

"Council member Chrysii is recognized."

The council chair didn't bother to look up at his conferee but continued instead to scan the results as they updated on his *phigitizers*, making occasional glimpses at the hunter standing stoically in the same spot to which he'd been directed.

Apparently, although it was forbidden to inculcate a non-Xylan, it was not *so* forbidden as to call for the discontinuance of this fascinating session and call for the authorities. Draugra's reckless gambit had apparently passed its first smell test. And although it was found to be a trifle malodorous, it was apparently not so smelly as to be completely offensive to the olfactory organ of the one who mattered the most--that being the council chair.

Having been recognized, the girl asking for leave to question Draugra looked at Bru in the same emotionless manner that a child might stare at a bug before using a stick to press it deep into the soil. Turning her attention suddenly to Draugra, she directed her question at the sorcerer.

"How much Xylan knowledge was transferred to this creature whom you refer to as a savage primate, knowing that such a transfer is forbidden in a lower order, resulting--as we know from past experimentation--in the expiration of the subject; although obviously not so in this case."

Draugra puffed up. This was the moment he'd long awaited. "You will find this savage to be capable of elaborating upon whatsoever topic you might desire. He has been successfully inculcated in science, physics, language, arcane studies... You ask how much of our knowledge did I transfer to the subject? I transferred all of it!"

Chrysii's dark eyes widened into twin, galactic pools.
"So much?"

18. Krahktohl

Quietly seething, Bru stood by patiently while the council members alternately whispered or hissed or shouted or debated as they argued the legitimacy of such a claim against the evidence on the *phigitizer* screens before them. Bru could care less about that. It made him furious that, despite the fact that the procedure Draugra performed on him was banned and known to be universally deadly, the selfish *phebüstart* pursued it anyway.

"These scan results, Draugra," Chrysii continued, "are highly unusual; but I am sure you have guessed that by now. I do not believe even you yet realize how remarkable they are. Are there many more of his kind? Where exactly did you find this creature? You say he comes from an unknown planet?"

"That," Draugra said with a smile on one side of his face, "is the million-*phollar* question, isn't it? His is a planet not yet mapped. I found it quite by accident."

"Yes, you said that already." The man who spoke was tall and gaunt, as was the sorcerer; thinning hair; totally unremarkable except perhaps regarding his lack of remarkability. "I wish to pose a question to Draugra."

The chairman sighed. "Council member Phylbyr is hereby recognized."

"Thank you, chairman. Draugra, I have it on good authority that you were tipped off by an individual to the existence of an unmapped world of which long-distance *phlebograffs* hinted might support life. As I am sure you are aware, this man--Krahktohl, a former associate of mine--went missing some two years ago together with his ship and survey data . . . that is about the same time you went missing yourself, is it not?"

Before Draugra could answer, Phylbyr continued.

"Do you deny that you were unaware of his explorations? Did you usurp Krahktohl's survey data and set out to claim his research? You as well as anyone know how exceedingly rare it is to discover a life-supporting planet, especially as far distant as another galaxy. The find was of inestimable value."

"Yet it sounds as though you've calculated it," Draugra insinuated nastily. "Only, we are not here today to discuss this Krahktohl person--whom I most certainly did not know--or this supposed survey of his, of which I also know nothing. Given that he was the honorable councilman's associate it seems a much more likely scenario that the councilman knows more about this Krahktohl's disappearance that would I--"

"You impertinent *phebiistart*--how dare you!" the other roared, storming to his feet.

"Rather, what we are here to discuss is the primate you see before you. I believe the scans have just completed. I hereby wish to present to the council evidence of the successful transfer of full Xylan knowledge to a sub-order . . . the first such to ever be successfully accomplished."

Bru turned his head this way and that to look into staring eyes, finding only one pair that interested him--Penelephii's. The stunning biologist sat beside Pylapharum in a loge set aside for non-council members who must be implicitly invited to observe a council session. Bru knew it was Draugra's request that they be present--Penelephii to impress her with her former lover's revelations and reinsert himself into her good graces, and Pylapharum to flaunt success in the face of a rival.

Again, the similarity to his own situation with Gla did not escape his notice except that it was his tribe Bru wished to impress and to whom he wished to appeal; but he also wished to win Oona, so there was that similarity as well to Draugra's current state.

"I submit that Krahktohl's discovery was stolen by this usurper and that Krahktohl was done away with!" the gaunt man retorted angrily. "To accuse me of doing away with a conferee is the height of--"

"Order, Councilman Phylbyr!"

"I wish to pose a question to the savage." The beautiful Chrysii again.

Smiling upon her--which was not at all hard to do--the council chairman nodded. "An excellent idea! If the primate is as filled with

8

Xylan knowledge as has been insinuated by candidate Draugra, a few questions shall suffice to bear out the claim. The scans do seem to indicate the presence of a savage of one of the lower orders; or at least, that is what the creature appears to have been at some point. Very strange indeed!"

"I would like myself to be recognized." Bru was reaching the point where he'd had enough. This was rapidly becoming a circus sideshow, whatever the *pthak* that was.

"Council member Chrysii has already been recognized. You shall remain under order until questioned where you may then speak in turn!"

The chairman banged his gavel, causing Bru to invest a few micro-seconds pondering what he'd specifically like to do with it.

"No."

Bru again.

"I will not stand here and obediently answer your questions like some sort of *phautomabot.* I told Draugra and now I'll tell you--my mind is so filled with knowledge that I could, without straining a single brain cell, stand here all day and ask questions of *you* that none of you could answer. You have your scans. Suffice to say that the knowledge Draugra claims to have crammed into my head is there, all interconnected for an ultimate understanding that every one of your scientists alive right now couldn't equal."

Bru jammed a finger toward the chairman. "For instance--you."

"I said you are to remain under order--" the chairman blustered.

"You suffer from *stoypalcydal;* the diagnosis is evident when one considers the slight stoop in your shoulders, the droop in your left eye, the manner in which you slump slightly forward in your chair and the garish tone of your skin. You've undoubtedly been told it's incurable by a bevy of experts. You fools don't know it, but it is the juice of the *phrape* being adversely affected during *Mine Borer* travel which causes this disorder in individuals predisposed to it. It's an extract of which you are apparently exceedingly fond. Cease all intake of the fruit of that vine during space travel and you shall be whole and hale in six months' time. If you don't, you'll be dead in less than a year."

"Now just how in the *Pthell* would you know that?"

"I know plenty. And speaking of Mine Boring technology, I know, from Draugra's memories that the council has been trying for decades to master the harvesting of dark energy to fuel the engines of *Mine Borer* craft which, although faster than *pthak*, are hideously expensive to operate. But no one has gotten close to a solution, have they? I tell you that until you learn to calculate the square root of negative *phi* and induce its value with the weight of a neutron nucleus you shall never accomplish it."

"But that's impossible--"

"No--I believe they are telling the truth!" Gorgeous Chrysii again.

"They?" quizzed Phlibion, her companion.

"Bru!" hissed Draugra.

"You can take the word of the smartest man in the cosmos." Bru smiled at Chrysii and studiously ignored the sorcerer.

"Which one of them is telling the truth," asked the chairman, confused, glancing from Chrysii to Phlibion to Draugra to Bru and then back to Chrysii.

The council members, whispering and arguing at Bru's astonishing statements, paused now to listen to the girl's reply. She looked up from her screens where she had been staring fixedly at Bru's scan results. She segued into a calculating glance at Draugra.

"Both of them," she replied.

19. Outlawry

"The scans are complete," Chrysii continued. "Ladies and *phentlemen*, you would do well to heed them."

En masse, the council bent their heads to their *phigitizers* where the final results of Bru's tests were being displayed.

"By the Teats of Lyra!" the chairman exploded, examining his screens. "Why, this would have caused pain beyond all endurance; off the charts, I would say. No, it's impossible. No man could have survived this--savage primate or no."

"I believe I know to what you refer." Draugra, a supercilious sneer now becoming evident on his lip, didn't bother this time asking permission of the chairman to speak. The session was beginning to break down into the chaos of incredulity; his smile deepened.

"These scans indicate that you not only inculcated the specimen with massive amounts of Xylan knowledge, but also with your own personal recording. That is, as you know, highly forbidden," Chrysii commented.

Although the expression on Council Member Chrysii's face was one of stern condemnation it seemed to be so out of a sense of duty rather than personal scorn. They were becoming fascinated--they just had yet to reach that point where they were able to admit it aloud to their conferees.

"Forbidden, yes, Councilman Chrysii, but look at what I have accomplished!" Draugra extoled in animated fashion. His extended finger swept the room, indicating the entire council body. "Your own experiments--before they became taboo--were always halted at the first hint of discomfort in a test subject, while I--"

"While you killed exactly how many hillmen before succeeding with me in your experiments?" Bru's grip on a hand rest caused the metal to protest. "*Pthell's* teeth, you *pthakking phebiistart*!"

"I myself would have possibly said . . . pushed the boundary," the chairman inserted.

Draugra openly grinned. It was beginning! Coming from the chairman, "pushing the boundary" was a far cry from, "a misdeed of the law". He had known with almost total certainty that they would be unable to resist the temptation of the type of knowledge Bru possessed. And he had been right! The interconnection between the disciplines was the paradigm toward which the Xylan council strove; and he had achieved it in Bru.

"Xylan brains have a limitation that prevent their being able to absorb enough raw data to reach that plateau beyond which would enable a race to make the next leap in intellectual progression," he said. "Bru's insightful observations just a moment ago prove that the savage has made that leap. Bru is now able to look across the entire spectrum of knowledge and make connections that are invisible to a thousand experts in as many fields--just as I suspected he would be."

Pressing a button, the chairman waited a moment. The silence, although brief, was thick as mammoth fur during that short interval. A door was heard to open and then four tall, burly men wearing the impedimenta and livery of guards entered. The chairman pointed at Bru.

"Take this man to the Q7 holding cell and await my summons before returning with him."

Bru saw that he was becoming an obstacle to the council's unfettered discussion. "You don't like it when the sub-man speaks his mind," he spat. "I'm finding that, although I assumed him to be a horrid outlier of your society, Draugra is instead exemplary of your kind."

"And I have told you for the last *pthakking* time to maintain silence until you are directed to speak," the chairman retorted nastily.

Firmly gripped by the guards, the plainsman was hustled out of the room and down a hall to a thick door which was manned by another quartet of guardsman; through this doorway they passed, and it was closed behind them.

***

"I can't abide how that man glowers!"

Draugra smiled at the chairman. "He can be . . . somewhat surly."

"Now we may speak more freely and hopefully without interruption," the chairman continued. "Draugra, I see within these scan results the evidence of transmutation, revisions to the bony structure are in evidence, and the cranial tissue, indications of a reshaping of the skull . . . the influx of knowledge in the subject has apparently spurred evolution to take place in the man's body."

The councilman's face was red with apparent indignancy--but then he suddenly relaxed.

"Who am I beguiling?" he asked. "This is too crucial, for Lyra's sake. Too much hinges on perfecting and perpetuating knowledge transfer of this kind. The people of the savage's world, as much as I hate to say it, must be brought to heel. Their ability to absorb knowledge on this scale . . . it's incredible, is what it is! And it's too important to allow outdated law to stand in the way of it."

The other council members, noting the reaction and the new direction of the chairman, also appeared to become less tense and critical. Many suddenly wore smiles where before they'd worn frowns of condemnation. There had been the law to consider, after all, but now...

"What was it the subject said a moment ago--the square root of negative *phi*?" asked Chrysii. "It is unbelievable!"

"Yes, induced by the weight of a neutron nucleus," another finished for her, grinning.

Draugra smiled. "*Now* you begin to see the possibilities. While I was stranded on that savage's home planet, he single-handedly developed new molecular structures from atoms that I knew nothing about that tested to exceed our own materials. It was quite fascinating to witness firsthand."

"Magnificent!" agreed Chrysii.

"The juice of the *phrape*," the chairman wondered aloud. The hunter had both diagnosed and prescribed for the man in only a few rapidly spat sentences. The chairman beamed, "Who would have dreamed that the cure would be so simple? All I have to do is lay off the *phwine* during Mine Boring. By Lyra, just think of the answers to other riddles that shall now be ours! It's limitless . . . boundless, I tell you!"

"I wonder what he knows about balding?" asked one aging member.

"We must have the law regarding non-Xylans stricken," Draugra hinted. He had them! Their comments assured him of it.

"And we shall," assured the chairman, "never fear. We hold great influence over the governing body."

"I propose a motion that we vote on the membership of Draugra to the council," purred pretty Chrysii. "We can certainly find a place for a man of his . . . discerning and enterprising acumen."

Her expression of disdain was missing now, replaced with a glow of excitement. Her eyes sought those of councilman Phlibion from whom she was accustomed to seeking private council meetings and held his gaze briefly. He smiled at her.

"We already have a full contingent!" Phylbyr exploded. "Even if we did not, I would still refuse to take part in any motion to vote this murderer into our illustrious number! There is no open seat! And the man has obviously broken numerous laws! Are all of you out of your collective minds?"

"We could increase the membership to twenty-three," proposed Chrysii.

"Somehow, Phylbyr, your tenacious obstinacy does not surprise me." It was Draugra who responded, rather than the chairman. "Chairman, if I may . . . I fear that Phylbyr may cause us trouble in the future."

The chairman, scowling, spun to face the senior council member who seemed intent on destroying this Lyra-granted opportunity because of his moral precepts and vaunted values.

"You're right, Draugra," he agreed, nodding. "That is precisely what he will do. I for one do not intend for this solution to be dragged out in the courts, although we control them. You're a *phidiot*, Phylbyr. Here is a planet full of brains that we can induce with the intelligences of a million scientists to find a path forward out of this stagnancy. You're a *pthakking* fool!"

This had gone far enough for the sorcerer. The time for words with this stupid *phoron* was over. The black device with which Bru had become familiar appeared in Draugra's hand; he flicked a setting on its side and leveled it upon Phylbyr.

Pylapharum, seated beside Penelephii, stood.

"Really, Draugra, has it come to this?" he objected. "I would love a seat on the council myself--so would Penelephii. But to pull a device on a council member? When he awakens, you will have changed nothing."

"If you are wise, Pylapharum, you will sit down and shut your mouth," Draugra threatened. "Unfortunately, that is no longer an option for Phylbyr; he won't be awakening from this."

Before Phylbyr could vocalize an exclamation of the surprise that was already making itself evident on his face, his face began disintegrating. Walking forward while continuing to spray the man with the lethal stream of energy, Draugra walked past Penelephii, offering the girl a smile while studiously ignoring Pylapharum and then continuing his way toward the evaporating councilman. Men and women on either side of and behind Phylbyr shouted and scrambled frantically from the path of Draugra's lethal ray.

"Dear, sweet blessed Lyra!" gasped the chairman, aghast at the site of one of his council members being converted into gore in their midst. He very nearly pressed the button to summon the guard, but thoughts of the inherent possibilities on Draugra's unknown planet again made up his mind for him. Also, he was unsure just how Draugra might react should he do so. He looked again toward Phylbyr; it was too late for the *phidiot*. No, they were committed now.

"To think that all this time we ignored the obvious path forward due to our own cowardice," he said, trying not to look again at poor Phylbyr. The older man could be an irritant, for sure, but he would have never wished *that* to befall him.

Daydreaming about those very possibilities made possible by Bru's successful inculcation of knowledge, one might have believed Chrysii and the others oblivious of the fact that a man was being turned into gravy on the other side of the room but for their occasional glances of morbid fascination.

"The laws!" one averred. "I for one might have done something similar long ago but for the *pthakking* laws! I always feared lest the results be calamitous, and I became publicly pilloried. But with this obvious success…"

"There will be other Phylbyrs," reminded Chrysii, continuing to watch until her former conferee had almost completely disappeared.

"We will deal with them similarly," said the chairman, showing resolve. "Anyway, our members have the ear of the government and the judicials. We shall revise the laws posthaste. A whole planet awaits our experimentation. This dark age of stagnancy will at long last lay behind us."

"I admit," offered Draugra, "that while I was marooned on that distant planet, I felt very little regard for the laws. I felt I would never have to face any consequences for my actions because it seemed at the time that I was hopelessly stranded. It was pure desperation that drove me to bring the savage back with me and attempt to sway the council of the errors of its ways; I almost let Bru go free. But to realize that the very thing we wished to accomplish was being stymied by our ban on non-Xylan knowledge transfer. I felt I needed to bring this to light."

"You were right to do so!" assured Phlibion.

In her mind, Chrysii was pondering Bru as though he were something good to eat and she was getting hungry. "He must be studied--at once. Much more deeply than these scans can provide. He must be interviewed by members of every facet of science and medicine. None may conceive the advances we shall make!"

"Our technologies have been stagnant for decades, but no more!" Phlibion nodded. "It shall take years, of course. So exciting!"

The others, now getting over the shock of seeing one of their own being disintegrated in the council chamber, were also talking excitedly. In the invitee's loge, Pylapharum didn't say anything more but only resumed his seat beside Penelephii. Given Draugra's seeming fascination with the girl and their known history, he

8

wondered if that would be safe in the future. Draugra was clearly mad. Pylapharum glanced at Penelephii only to find her staring in fascination at Draugra.

20. Maintenance Man

With a council guard on either side of him grasping him by his arms Bru reentered the chambers, dragged hence by his sentinels in answer to the chairman's summons. Upon the council members faces were mixed emotions but the overarching sentiment he perceived was a resolve that made him feel like he was a tasty dish being eyed by a café full of hungry customers.

Bru's brows met in a scowl. "Draugra. I think we're finished here. Your promise?"

He was aware by this point that it was a long shot. Based on what he had heard these people did not intend to let him go--ever. Like starving beasts tossed a mammoth's hind quarter, they would sink their teeth into him and never let go. It was the next statement from the chairman that caused him to assume a crouch like a wild animal.

"It is apparent that this planet, wherever it is, has a supply of indigenous peoples capable of being escalated to the levels we wish. While it would be better if we ourselves could become these vessels of all knowledge where the various disciplines may then be cross-referenced with an understanding that is completely encompassing, we already know that there are limits where we are concerned. Your people, Bru, do not seem to have that same limitation."

"Maybe not all of us; I'm an exception. Did *pthak*-face tell you how many hillmen he killed in his experiments?" The low growl that escaped Bru' lips he couldn't have prevented had he wished. It was the primal reaction of the beast turning at bay to protect its herd, the savage his mate and offspring, or in this case, a genius his world. His spring from the handrail was executed with such force that it bent the *strongium* of which it was made, acting as a springboard and speeding him like a bullet straight for Draugra.

It mattered not to Bru that the sorcerer or some other might bring a device to bear and disintegrate him, as Draugra had with the hillmen. Bru was a primal man, built for speed and strength and in possession of both, while the Xylan was a pantywaist of the first water, and in possession of neither. Draugra's arm had barely begun to twitch in reaction to the savage sailing the short distance through the air toward him when Bru's extended right hand engulfed the other's throat. Bru's left hand simultaneously grasped and ripped the black device from the Xylan's effete grip.

Bru bashed Draugra's head two or three times against the stone floor and then stood, leaving the sorcerer lying stunned beneath him. The hunter glanced at the device in his hand before leveling it upon Draugra.

"You *pthakker*," he muttered.

And he pressed a button on the side of the device.

Bedlam erupted in the council chamber. With a borderline mega-genius with the physique of a forest god and the strength of a bodybuilder preparing to slaughter them with a few sideways swipes of the device he was holding in one of his ham-fisted, primate paws, several made hasty grabs for their own devices; in this they were stymied.

"Cut it," Bru growled; motioning with the business end of his device, he directed them to raise their hands where he could see them.

The hunter was seriously pondering giving them a taste of what he'd just given Draugra but the thought of leveling a device upon Penelephii was nearly as distasteful to him as though she were his own, dear Oona. He knew his confounding feelings to be but the result of Draugra's memories, but still . . . they were as real to him as though they were his own emotions.

"Bru?" The girl had barely breathed his name.

He knew that if he met her eyes with his own that his resolve would falter. Bru suspicioned that Draugra's feelings for the girl ran deeper than even the sorcerer realized--the biologist really had it bad for the girl. The ironic thing was that, having the biologist's memories--and by extension, his feelings--embedded in his brain also turned Bru into a weak-kneed sap; and Penelephii was just the sort of girl who would exploit that scenario without a second thought.

"Quiet, Penelephii, and let me think," he said, trying not to sound too harsh.

"There's nowhere for you to go; nowhere to turn," said the chairman. "Wherever you hide, you will be found. You won't make it to a space port."

Bru happened to disagree with the chairman's assessment. Sifting through Draugra's memories of the council chamber, he recalled an ante-room, reserved for private audiences with members of the council. It was small, but he felt it would work for his intended use.

***

Bru missed walking through waist high grasses in early summer or sucking on those last icicles of late spring before longer days and warming weather caused them to disappear for months. He missed the lake, the rivers, and the shelters of his people. He missed Oona.

"She's probably mated with Gla by now, or been vaporized by that *pthakking* volcano," he muttered under his breath; both thoughts were painful. He was currently walking the low lit passages of a maintenance level of the high rise structure to which Draugra had brought him.

Bringing the sorcerer's device to bear in the council chamber a few *tarts* earlier, he had quickly ushered the guards and council members into the ante-chamber, confiscated their devices and then *phused* the door lock; their devices he had them toss into a pile which he then turned into a stain on the council floor using the *phuse* setting once more, and being careful not to inhale any of the fumes that this action left floating around the chamber. The Xylans were unhappy with this sudden turn of events but of course Bru could care less. He had enjoyed waving the device in the chairman's face and watching the man cringe; but he had avoided looking Penelephii in the eye.

After closing and smelting the lock on the outer chamber door the hunter immediately stepped into a sanitation turret and descended several levels. Although reaching the planet's surface and hiding out in the wilds was an almost overpowering, instinctual urge which the plainsman in him found difficult to resist, he had no intention of doing so. It would not help his case to wander the wilderness of Xyla; nor would it save Oona and his people.

9

2

Bru knew from Draugra's memories that all Xylan vessels were equipped with sensors capable of detecting human lifeforms; from the safety and comfort of their flyers, his captors would have located him with consummate ease if he was running amok in the wilds. Remaining in the building where humanity abounded would make him much more difficult to pinpoint because they would have to resort to their facial recognition sensors; and Bru happened to know that these were not located in the sanitation and ventilation systems.

The maintenance man he happened upon paid him almost no mind at all; not that it would have mattered if he had. Bru needed garb that would not attract attention so that he might slip with ease through the residential areas he had it in mind to visit; the uniform this man was wearing would work nicely. The fellow looked up politely as they were about to pass by one another in the passage.

Smiling when he recognized Bru's council garb, the man began to comment, "Good day to you sir--"

If the man's eyes registered the speeding, hammer-like fist that busted his lips into his teeth and drove his head into the wall along the passage he would probably never be able to recollect it when he awakened later. Bru grasped the man's unconscious form about the waist and darted into a storage room where he hastily stripped the fellow, donning the maintenance clothes over his own; one never knew--he might have need again of the sciency garments with which Draugra had clothed him.

After he exited the storage room Bru picked up the articles the man had been carrying and continued walking in the direction in which he had already been proceeding. He smiled. He had shrewdly surmised where the Xylans would seek him once they escaped from the council chambers; the unfortunate thing for them was that he had no intention of going there.

By the time they were flocking to the launch stations atop the high rise buildings, the savage plainsman would be multiple levels below and far away from the council chamber. It was, he admitted, a logical choice for them to make. The man wished to escape Xyla and would naturally gravitate to a space port where thousands of these vessels would be lying in wait. And there *they* would lie in wait for him. Well, they could wait till *Pthell* unthawed. He had other plans.

With the specific piece of gear that he had need of in hand, it was to the residential section that his feet now carried him. In the passages through which he traipsed, and in all of the many enormous rooms and chambers filled with concourses of Xylans through which he waded elbow to elbow, would be those who sought him. For he knew the council wouldn't base their entire gambit on one assumption. They would have those out seeking him amongst the unknowing populace and his facial scans would be plastered across all of the public *phigitizers*.

Unfortunately for them, Bru was not parading about with his face exposed where it might be recognized by a camera or searcher. Instead, he had sought out a member of those whom he recalled from his collection of Draugra's memories who would have upon his person a certain piece of equipment which Bru could use to effectively disguise his features, but in an unobtrusive manner that would not otherwise call attention to him.

The maintenance man he had knocked senseless had been in possession of a standard safety shield which, when activated, suffused the wearer with a protective field. The field wasn't so evident that it would be noticed by the casual observer but would distort the lines of facial features enough to avoid being detected by the *phautoscanners*--the facial recognition system which was embedded throughout the city.

He grinned when he thought how unwise the council was that in the section from which he had escaped, it was devoid of these *phautoscanners*. If they had been installed in the council's chambers and halls, they would have seen him dart into the sanitation turret and possibly guessed what he was up to. Being members of the planet elite had its perks and being able to come and go untracked was apparently one of them.

Bru entered an area which saw a decrease in the crowds of the public squares and bazaars. When he reached the rooms that were his destination, he utilized Draugra's device to gain access. Really, they put all their eggs in one nest as far as he was concerned with these devices; they used them for literally everything. With this in hand he could inculcate a primitive pygmy to a basic level of intellect, torture him, disintegrate him, make purchases in the commercial district, activate the safety protocols on a star craft and many other things--such as enter the device owner's flat like he was currently doing.

Upon entering the suite, he was confronted by a startled housekeeper whom he nearly scared out of her scanty maid's attire when he just walked in unannounced. He smiled at her disarmingly, but he had already deactivated his safety shield; as luck would have it, at that very moment his face was being prominently displayed on a nearby *phigitizer*. He also smiled because the girl was easy on the eyes; Draugra had excellent taste in service.

"Who are you? What do you want? Please don't hurt me!" the girl stammered while backing away fearfully. Her eyes darted to the *phigitizer* on the wall and then back to Bru's face. An announcer was just describing Bru as having disintegrated councilman Phylbyr; no mention was made of his assault on Draugra for some reason.

"That is a lie, so don't believe it. I'm not the one who dissolved that councilman. And I've no intention of harming you; or anyone else for that matter. I just want to go the *pthak* home."

"But you have the master's device," she stammered; she was looking at the menacing, black device in Bru's hand.

The savage guessed what she was thinking; that only with the owner's device might he have thus easily gained entry to these apartments so that must be Draugra's device he was holding. Bru could understand why this might make her fearful. She probably thought that he had done away with her master and was now fibbing about not intending to harm her in order to get information out of her before disintegrating her with the device's *phatomizer* setting. The girl's voice had a pitiful tremor to it that made the hunter feel ashamed. The girl was obviously fearful for her life.

"Look, I'll prove I'm not going to hurt you. I'm going to let you walk right out of here in just a *tart*. First, give me your device," he demanded. He reached out his hand, brooking no argument.

95

He could have let her leave right then but knew she would tell the first constabulary she ran across about him. He could have blasted her with the *phatomizer* or put her in a coma with the *comapthyzer*. But he had an idea that might make her choose not to inform on him, and that would not force him to blast an innocent girl with any sort of ray--deadly or otherwise. In the end it was going to be her choice whether she informed on him or not.

Her hands were trembling when the poor girl handed him a device which was similar to Draugra's, but a more basic variant. Bru saw that it had none of the deadly, built-in ray dispersers or knowledge transferal equipage--which one could use to learn micro bits of information when time was of the essence--features which were only found on scientists' devices who explored in the name of the council. Hers was a simpler device for the run-of-the-mill civilian to conduct business and secure his or her holdings.

Bru opened a tiny panel on it. "May I borrow one of your hair pins?"

He pointed to her coif and smiled to reassure her. Still doubtful--but now curious--she removed a barrette to a cascade of midnight black tresses and reached it to him. Utilizing the pin as a touch control and a bridge between a couple of circuits on her device, Bru next executed a procedure on Draugra's device followed by another minute adjustment to hers and then reached her device back to her.

The sorcerer's memory scans had not been quite up to date, having been last updated about three years prior, and so the hunter had no knowledge or memories of the housekeeper. She was probably employed by a service; for all he knew, Draugra may have never met her, having been absent for two years. As Bru reached her device back to her, he said, "There you are, Miss…?"

"I am Phonna," she supplied, after a moment's hesitation. If he intended to do away with her then why waste time changing the settings on her device? And why ask her name?

"Phonna," he repeated, "a pretty name. I apologize for the inconvenience in asking this of you, Miss Phonna, but if you will, I now require that you vacate these premises and to please tell no one that you've seen me. If you don't do as I ask, I shall remove

9

the small adjustment I made to your device just now which, when you see it, should convey to you the depth of my gratitude for any inconvenience I might have caused you. Do you understand?"

Not understanding at all, and with her brows contracted in a worried frown, the girl nodded anyway.

"Excellent!" Bru replied. "Now, if you will?" Bru nodded toward the door and swept one hand toward it in a gesture that could not be misinterpreted.

Somewhat reassured--but also not requiring any further invitation--the girl took a light wrap she had hanging on a hook in the foyer as she passed by it and quickly fled, closing the door behind her without another word. Once she was out of the apartment, she wasted no time in hurrying down the hallway before the large man in her master's apartment might change his mind. Becoming curious about what he had done to her device, she pulled it out and examined it, half fearing he had somehow turned it into an explosive. Such was not the case.

"Holy Lyra!" she exclaimed, smiling.

The stranger had eliminated all of her debts and maxed out her bank credits with an enormous sum that, unbeknownst to her, he had removed from all of the sorcerer's accounts in a manner that would be untraceable, leaving Draugra without a *phollar* to his name. She now had enough credits that she would never have to work again. When she passed an armed, security team several *tarts* later accompanied by a large group of people who were all hurrying in the direction from which she had just come, she didn't say a word.

***

Bru wasted no time after the maid vacated the premises, but instantly utilized the apartment's *phlevelavator* to proceed to the next floor below--the flat's built-in VDS, or <u>V</u>essel <u>D</u>ocking <u>S</u>tation. Here sat Draugra's *Z2 Plasma Folder,* the same ship that Bru had repaired almost single-handedly.

"Just what I was looking for," he sighed when he saw it.

He was quite relieved to find the craft here. He had noticed that it was missing from the landing pad at the science building the morning after they had arrived when he breakfasted with Penelephii and Pylapharum; Draugra had left it there temporarily, being in a hurry to get Bru into custody of the council. Just guessing, Bru assumed that Draugra had returned later and flew it to his personal dock which Bru knew about from the sorcerer's memories. Not everyone in Xylan society possessed such an arrangement; it was a status symbol of which Draugra was quite proud.

Utilizing Draugra's device, he commanded the ship to drop its boarding ramp so he could enter. Assuming the *philot's* chair he rapidly began running his hands across the control surfaces as though he was as familiar with them as he was Oona's face. Actually, he *was* that familiar with them. Draugra's memories and the knowledge imparted to him via the instructor-helms had made him as fluent with the ship's controls as though he had worked with them every day of his life.

He was finishing some pre-flight settings when the *phlevelavator* swooshed open to admit a full coterie of security and council members, all of whom were clearly visible through the view screens. He saw the chairman--and Chrysii and Phlibion were there, too, together with several of the others. And there was good old Pylapharum.

He could see that they were all shouting at him, but he didn't bother to actuate the external *phaudio* system; he had no desire nor need to hear what they had to say. He had to admit that he was surprised, though, that they had so quickly guessed that he would come here.

Continuing to ignore them, he actuated the shields which effectively prevented any attempt to board the vessel or damage it; he brought up the vessel's coordinate history. Next, he selected its latest recorded trajectory; utilizing the controls to set this as its destination, he settled on a duplicate course that would return him to the precise location in the mountains of his world where Draugra had landed this ship two years prior.

"Oona's necklace had better be right where Draugra said he left it, " he muttered. "And that volcano had better not have erupted

9

yet." He glanced out the view screens at the shouting Xylans. "Or I'm going to come back here and kick some *pthazz*."

Bru stabbed the button to initiate take-off.

21. Drain the Brain

Although the manner in which the antique *Plasma Folder* leaped through space was extraordinary, anything short of instantaneous must be considered as traveling at a crawl by the impatient plainsman. Yet given that the coordinates of his homeworld were stored only in Draugra's vessel's navigation system, he'd had little choice but to take this particular ship. He would have preferred to have stolen one of the faster *Mine Borers* but hadn't had the time to transfer the navigation information from one ship to another. And too, those ships were under heightened security at the time.

Having been unconscious for the entire journey to Xyla and therefore having no way of knowing how long the trip had taken, he settled on a complex project to tinker with to kill time. With the ship set on *phautomatic*, he proceeded to the science bay and retrieved the last helmet that Draugra had used upon him--the one that contained Draugra's memories; just looking at the educator-helm made him want to retch.

"Now, let's just take a look at your innards and see what makes you tick," he muttered, taking up a complex tool.

Rushing through the hunter's brain was the knowledge of countless scientists and inventors. That was fine; he could handle the cascade of ideas this created in his mind; enjoyed it, even. He had so many ideas nowadays that he considered the pitifully few thoughts he'd had when he was but a simple plainsman as basically not thinking at all by comparison.

He could even handle the memories of two uniquely different men, although one of them was admittedly a man he detested with every fiber of his being. He was torn on this, though. Having the man's memories stored in his brain, and feeling as though they were his own thoughts, often caused him to try to justify the sorcerer's selfish motivations.

"Yuck," he said aloud; the thought of justifying anything that bear's rear-end said or did was distasteful to him. He was also repulsed with how the actions and thoughts of Draugra often paralleled and reminded him of his former self. He intended to be rid once and for all of these sensations.

1

Being both on the inside in possessing the sorcerer's memories and the outside by his own observations of Draugra's relationship with the beautiful Penelephii had proven to be a unique situation. Bru knew from Draugra's memories that the sorcerer was hopelessly in love with the beautiful Xylan biologist. He also knew from his observations of the girl's body language that Draugra didn't stand a chance in *Pthell* with her. And when Bru wasn't focusing on his own memories, he would begin to--again, somewhat sickeningly--empathize with the man.

"*Pthak* that!" he swore. "You deserve it, Draugra. You totally deserve whatever she dishes out."

Bending over his instruments Bru began carefully and laboriously disassembling the bulky educator-helm in which Draugra had stored his memories a few years prior. Bru grimaced, recalling the last time he had this helmet over his head and face, the awful nightmare he had experienced of Oona slowly sliding her arm out of his throat; the thought that this same umbilical had once slid down Draugra's throat as well didn't make the proposition any more appealing.

Steeling his resolve, he continued to labor as his ship folded space and closed the distance to his home, eventually exposing the complex circuitry and memory banks within the helmet. Not stopping there, he traced the conduits, connecting the helmet to a *comphuter* in the tiny, on-board laboratory, and began rewriting the code that embedded the stored memories in one's mind.

"You can cancel a sound with a sound--so why not a memory with a memory?" he theorized.

Placing that helmet over his head--and knowing what was to come--was the worst part. It was like purposely choosing to experience a nightmare that caused one to awaken in a cold sweat.

"I must have Oona's face and form to cancel the other," he muttered.

Even knowing it was coming, he still gagged when the umbilical shot down his throat and the *phem-phlaps* clapped over his eyes and ears…

***

The trip was accomplished with incredible rapidity for the Xylan science was indeed daunting. Having been distracted with reprogramming Draugra's educator-helm with the goal of reversing the process in order to remove the sorcerer's memories from his brain, in a shorter time than Bru believed possible he was sailing past the moon of his world where he was able to catch intriguing glimpses of its mysterious surface before it disappeared to stern.

Now he was staring down upon a beautiful, blue world against a backdrop of impenetrable black. It was--with the exception of Oona--the loveliest thing he had ever seen in his life. Still set on *phautomatic*, the vessel entered an intercept course with the planet and began an approach.

The man stared at the vistas before him, memorizing as much as possible; he knew that this would be the one and only time he would ever see his world from this perspective, so his countenance was one of deep appreciation. He didn't dilly dally, though; there was still an imminent eruption to consider. The ship pierced the vapors of the firmament and angled on a course that was a precise duplicate of Draugra's. Bru stared ahead until his eyes burned from his fixed, unblinking gaze.

"There it is!" he exclaimed, thumping an armrest on the *philot's* chair.

He instantly recognized the ranges before him although he had never before viewed them from this angle or altitude. Having always gazed upward at them though fear-filled eyes, he now smiled upon their stellar beauty. One of them was The Fang of Tysk, a jagged, icy peak his people pointed out to scare children who were being naughty, claiming it to be the fang of a vast tiger that lay sleeping beneath the ground; Bru recalled his own mother scaring the *Pthell* out of him when he was young with threats of Tysk coming to get him if he didn't straighten up.

Smoke and fumes were drifting from its immense depths.

"Tysk awakens; Tysk is angry!" He grunted the words in the old tongue of the people. It felt good and clean, somehow, to speak the simple language of the plainsmen instead of the gilded tongue of the Xylans.

1

It was now that Bru must be the most vigilant. If the volcano had not yet erupted, and earthquakes had not destroyed the stone shelf upon which Draugra had formerly landed his ship, then Bru intended to land there and retrieve the necklace he had made for Oona and which she had later gifted him upon his banishment.

But if the volcano had already erupted and his people no longer existed? He couldn't dwell for long upon that scenario. If such was the case he might, in the depths of misery and desolation, destroy himself and the ship in the core of the volcano; he just wasn't sure he could continue completely alone--without Oona, and without his tribe.

"If Oona is gone, I might follow her into darkness," he muttered. "Or wander the wastes." He thought for a moment. "Or I might return to Xyla." He frowned. "They won't like it if I do."

Having dropped in elevation to a height where he could see more clearly, he strained his eyes toward the lake and the plains. With his hands moving familiarly over the controls, he began taking readings, scanning for lifeforms. He was soon rewarded with evidence of several groups of hillmen in the mountains and foothills.

He was thrilled to see signs of the hillmen as it meant the plainsmen were probably safe. But then he grimaced when he considered that many of these hillmen would be obliterated in the coming eruption. At one time he would have thrilled that this doom was to fall upon the enemies of his people. But with the inheritance of knowledge that was now his had also come enlightenment. No longer did he despise the hillmen. Instead, understanding and compassion had taken the place of fear and hate. Still, there wasn't enough time to warn them of their impending fates.

"They wouldn't believe me, anyway," he reasoned. "Just like I would not have believed them if they were to come to the Seven Rivers Tribe bearing this same, bizarre tale."

When he found a dense population of humanoids out upon the plains where he had last seen his tribe his face split in a wide grin.

All thoughts of the doomed hillmen fled as he nearly lost his mind to the flood of relief pouring over him.

"There they are! They're still alive. *Pthak*, what a relief! Oona-- there's still time!"

Thoughts of ending his life in the volcano or wandering the world alone were banished; and no longer did he contemplate a vengeful return to Xyla for which those of Xyla should be eternally thankful. Monitoring the scanners and sensors and keeping his eyes peeled out the forward viewscreens, Bru watched closely as the vessel duplicated Draugra's descent toward the stone shelf below the crater rim. He was relieved to see that the wide ledge was still visible through the vapor and smoke. There was considerably more rubble lying about, indicating further seismic activity, but otherwise it looked the same as when he and Draugra were last here.

Assuming manual control of the vessel he began dropping the ship, wishing to deviate from its recorded landing path and set it down further away from the unstable cliff which had partially collapsed once before and caused the extensive damage he repaired. Although he had never flown in his life, the primitive hunter executed a perfect manual landing, thanks to the recorded knowledge of the many aeronauts he carried about in his head.

Shutting down the vessel, Bru stood to debark, but paused, looking about the cabin. Should he return for the vessel after he retrieved the necklace, or leave the ship here to be destroyed by the volcano? He didn't want to frighten his people by landing too near their shelters in an object that might later be used to frighten children into submission, for Lyra's sake.

Recalling his own terrors when he had been confronted and captured by Draugra helped him make up his mind with finality. His world wasn't ready for an instant dose of such advanced technology; it should be introduced slowly. The better part of wisdom would be to allow the ship to be rendered into its base atoms in the coming blast.

"Poor Draugra. I don't think I ever saw such an expression of surprise as when you let him have it with his own device."

Bru spun to face the owner of the voice. There in the doorway, holding a leveled device, stood Penelephii.

1

22. Surprise

"Penelephii! But . . . how?"

The girl smiled an enticing smile that not long ago would have made Bru's heart to skip a few beats and then pound in anticipation and cause him to forget that she was holding a lethal device pointed at his chest.

"Hello, Bru. Surprised to see me?"

There were those charming dimples. "In fact, I am," he admitted.

"The council," the girl purred silkily, "initially assumed that you would race for the fastest ship on Xyla. But it made more sense to me that you would head for the only vessel with the stored flight path to your planet. By the time they figured that out they'd lost precious time and when they arrived you and I were already aboard. Not being forced to take a roundabout way like you, I arrived first, entering Draugra's apartments by a private door I'd used in the past. I boarded the ship without Draugra's maid ever knowing I was within a hundred *phmiles* of her."

"Well, that was clever of you. What do you want, Penelephii?" His entire body had become tense with coiled energy; he forced himself to relax. He stood there, appearing as at ease as any man who was speaking to a maid for whom he had feelings. Her smile no longer fooled him, though; the girl was dangerous. Surreptitiously, he moved his hand toward the side pocket where Draugra's device lay.

But Penelephii wasn't so easily fooled. "That's far enough Bru. Just keep those hands away from those pockets and where I can see them. That's a good boy."

At a gesture from her he raised his arms away from his waist and crossed them over his chest. Well, *pthak*! He would just have to wait and see how this played out. If an assumption on which he was gambling *didn't* go exactly as he hoped, he seriously risked ending up like all those poor hillmen the sorcerer disintegrated.

"Where Draugra failed, I intend to succeed, Bru," Penelephii was telling him. "Even should the experimentations to create super brains to boost our stagnant knowledge fail, there is still an entirely unexplored, life-supporting world here to claim--they're quite rare, actually. But you know this, already--I keep forgetting! So, you also know that I win either way."

"I think the council knows to whom the honor of discovering this planet belongs, Penelephii."

"Yes, poor Krahktohl. Honestly, I have no idea what Draugra did with the man or his ship. Quite the mystery, there! But I bet I can guess where Krahktohl's *phradionic* fuel bars went. Krahktohl had a *Z2 Plasma Folder,* too," she winked. "Those plasma fuel bars don't come cheap! Insofar as who gets credit for discovering this planet, though, I'll be the one holding the coordinates. And at the end of the day, that's really all that counts."

Bru shrugged. "True enough. I spoke sufficiently with your council to understand how they reason. And you know what they say about possession and all that. But none of that really matters to me, Penelephii. I only wish to save my people from certain calamity."

The girl pretended to pout. "Oh, I know, Bru--and I am sorry! But now that I've verified Draugra's claims about this world I must return to Xyla immediately. I'm sure you can understand that there just isn't time to visit your friends this trip. There are still a million questions our scientists will want to ask you."

Not by the flicker of a single eyelash did Bru reveal how relieved he was to her say that they wanted to question him on Xyla. His assumption was going to go in the direction he'd hoped. Her statement meant that when she was finished toying with him that she didn't intend to kill him with her disintegrator. Rather, she planned to render him unconscious for the long haul back to Xyla. So, he wasn't to end up like a disintegrated hill man after all.

"You can make new friends here later," she quasi-promised him. "I tapped into the ship's *comphuter* and saw the results of the scans you ran as we were landing. They left me dizzy with excitement. This place! There are tribes of humanoids dotting nearly the entirety of the continent--and that's just this one

1

landmass! I can only imagine what further discoveries lay in store. I shall assume Council Chair in no time!"

Increased rumblings beneath them made themselves noticeable, causing both to glance out the cabin's windows at the surrounding walls of stone rising above them. A fissure in a perpendicular cliff not too far from them opened while they were looking at it, causing a cascade of shattered stone. Luckily, the landslide was far enough away from the ship to cause Bru little concern. Penelephii only smiled, seemingly unafraid by the proximity of death.

"You chose wisely when you landed, Bru! I imagine that Draugra did not, resulting in the damage his ship suffered."

"You guessed that right."

"I also guessed early on that it was not he who repaired the vessel, but that it was you. He later admitted as much."

The hunter's brows came together in perplexity. "He admitted that? Must have been while I was locked up in your council cage."

The girl laughed easily. "Yes, sorry about that. I saw a look of scorn on your face during the council meeting that spoke more eloquently than anything you could have said aloud; I figured he had threatened you into silence. Draugra lied about pretty much everything, didn't he?"

"He's a prevaricator of the highest rank, that's for sure. If you have such a low estimation of him then why did you date him for all those months?"

"Poor Bru! You're really are just along for the ride, aren't you? I thought he was going somewhere, that's why! As it turned out, I was right; but by then I had already given up on him. He was missing for two *pthakking* years! Speaking of which, he is going to be furious when I return. I might be forced to set the same example of him as he did with Phylbyr."

The cold, calculating manner in which the girl casually spoke of disintegrating her former lover sickened Bru to his core. These people! They came from a knowledgeable and a supposedly illuminated society--certainly far more advanced than anything the former, simpler Bru could have ever imagined; and yet at heart they were as base and greedy as a hill man.

The girl smiled one of her sultry smiles for which she was justifiably famous, further driving home the amazement he felt at her peoples' level of depravity. They would do or say anything to beguile and bend people to their wills.

"So, Draugra gave you his memories, didn't he?"

"You guessed that, too?"

"I didn't have to; he told us. Not that it would have taken a Plasma Folder scientist to figure that one out. And certainly not after you mentioned Pylon's outer moon! Every time I smiled at you, you blushed and looked away." The girl pursed her lips provocatively. "I sensed Draugra's memories of me wasn't all that was embedded in that pretty head of yours. You have his feelings, as well . . . don't you, Bru?"

The question was breathed out in a manner that caused the plainsman to squirm. Was it from embarrassment that he writhed? Or shame--feeling that he had somehow betrayed Oona with his former feelings for this girl from another world? Either way, it was true--he had been the inheritor of not only Draugra's knowledge and memories, but also of the sorcerer's affection for the girl.

Only now he was no longer a slave to those implanted affections. Because he had ripped those engravings from his mind by their filthy roots with his adjustments to the educator helm, although it had gagged him to do so--literally and figuratively. He just couldn't let Penelephii guess as much.

"What I don't understand is why you didn't kill Draugra when you had the chance?" she broke into his thoughts. "No one would have blamed you; I certainly wouldn't miss him. Had I been in your shoes, I would have given him a taste of *pthatomyzer* instead of resorting to the coma setting; *Pthell*, that's probably what he did to old Krahktohl."

"I've no doubt you would've killed him," Bru agreed. "But I was content to use the *comapthyzer*. I'm not like you, Penelephii, and although he gave me his memories, I'm not like Draugra, either. I'm a simple hunter. My people respect life. We become animated at times and fight amongst ourselves, that's true; but we would lay down our lives to protect our own. Your arcane knowledge and Draugra's memories don't define me. I'm no murderer. When I kill it's justified, in honest combat, where I can feel a measure of pride in defeating a worthy foe--not a helpless one. There's nothing respectable at all about disintegrating an unarmed man."

"Oh my, don't we have some antiquated notions!" The girl's sparkling, irreverent laughter sounded as infectious and invigorating as it did when he first encountered her on Xyla. Luckily for him, it no longer caused his heart rate to spike.

"Since you care so little for Draugra, then what of Pylapharum? You and he seemed rather close; I know it gave Draugra several intense moments," he grinned.

"Pylapharum? That fool? He doesn't have the grit. And Draugra can't be trusted. Now a man like you, Bru..." the girl insinuated seductively.

She eyed his magnificent physique from head to toe like she was eyeing a perfectly grilled steak. She flashed the hunter one of her winning smiles that she'd used a thousand times to mold men to her will. If Bru loved her half as much as had Draugra, then she was already as good as sitting in the council chair's seat. With such a man at her side almost anything would be possible. If he didn't love her, no matter; she had her device, and she had the ship with the planet coordinates. She would get what she wanted regardless.

"You mentioned earlier about who will be next to chair the council," Bru said. "I myself lean more toward them choosing Chrysii."

"Chrysii?" Penelephii's soft lips tensed into a rigid line. That was apparently not a contingency she had considered.

Well, that certainly did the trick.

"Yes," continued Bru; it was too late to stop now. "I mean, she has everything going for her, right? Looks, intelligence, sophistication; she's already on the council, while you are not. I found her line of questioning to be particularly astute; quite the indication of erudition. It makes me feel she would make a fine chairperson; not that you wouldn't, obviously."

"Chrysii can kiss my *pthazz*!" Snarling like a saber tooth, the vexed girl kicked a navigation seat and set it spinning.

He really had hit a nerve.

"She did nothing to deserve a seat on the council. Because her father was once the sitting chair everyone thinks she should be, too. Everything is always handed to her with no effort on her part. She was the first to wear the Level Two instructor-helm when we were girls, the first of us to sail to Albion, the first to be asked to join the council--she always has to be first!"

"I can see where that would be frustrating," he agreed." I myself always had to struggle and put in the hard work for the precious little appreciation I received, just like you."

Bru had guessed that the girl harbored old resentments, seeming to recall her mentioning Chrysii negatively to Draugra when they were seeing each other. He could recall no details of it, however. Since reverse-engineering the educator-helm that held the sorcerer's memories, he could actually recall very little of Draugra's life now, his redesign having done a splendid job of removing the bulk of it from his brain.

And of what little remained, it was now Oona's face that he saw as he made love on Pylon's outer moon and other beautiful and exotic locales. And for this he was glad. It meant that no longer did Penelephii hold sway over his heart as she had while on Xyla; he just couldn't let her know that.

Bru's comments had done a splendid job of incensing the girl. She was waving her device around erratically, causing Bru to duck twice when it swept in his direction, being unsure of what setting it was on. If she accidentally squeezed off a blast with the *pthatomyzer* that would end his career right here and now. He hoped that didn't happen.

He had set out to distract her, and in this he had finally been successful. While her back was briefly turned to him, he slid one hand into a side pocket and retrieved his device, making a quick adjustment to its current settings as it cleared his clothing. At the sound of the soft *snick* this produced, the girl spun, raising her black device and leveling it straight at his chest.

23. A Ticklish Situation

"That's far enough, Bru!" The girl's eyes reflected steely glints of determination and the hunter knew she would not hesitate to press the button on her device. "I should have guessed you would become as corrupted as Draugra!"

"As corrupt as Draugra? Hardly. I think you're judging me on your own merits--not mine. You did point yours at me first, you might recall."

The man glanced casually at his own device and then slowly and purposely raised his arm. As he extended it toward the girl her eyes became as wide as a Xylan ten-*phollar* coin.

"Bru! Don't forget that you love me! You can't fire that device at me!"

The hunter wasn't confused about where his feelings lie any longer and had no trouble thinking of Oona, her dear face and form springing instantly before his mind's eye with sparkling clarity.

"Actually, I can."

But the girl was quicker. Before he finished speaking, she spat, "I warned you."

Bru felt the *comapthyzer* waves of her device coursing through his brain as his body became awash with waves of giddy, ticklish sensations, causing him to grin like a loon.

Penelephii's eyes were wide with surprise when she released the button on her device. As though unsure if she'd had the button pressed completely, she brought her device to bear again. Once more the ticklish waves bathed the plainsman in their giddy energies. To the hunter, it felt as though a dozen children were tickling him unmercifully. Finally laughing outright, he begged her to desist.

With surprise writ all over her face, she managed, "Why are you not collapsing? Why are you not insensible? Draugra said he rendered you unconscious when he captured you--*and* when he took you to Xyla!"

Bru grinned, relieved on more than one account, the first being the device setting for which he had guessed Penelephii would opt; his gamble had paid off.

"When Draugra captured me, he used the sleep-inducing *somnipthyzer* setting, not the coma setting you just used. I'd say he did so from his early experiences with the hillmen. He would have started off using the *comapthyzer* on them and quickly discovered that it doesn't work on the people of my world. Do you recall Draugra mentioning that I have no *Phidula Phortex*? The *comapthyzer* works on that area of the brain--of the <u>Xylan</u> brain, that is. It has no effect whatsoever on my kind . . . but for a ticklish sensation, that is."

"*Pthak*! Blast Draugra! He said he brought you to Xyla unconscious for the entire trip!" she fumed. "He lied! He's always lying about something!"

"He actually didn't lie in this instance; he did take me to Xyla unconscious. But he rendered me in that state with the electrical restraints he placed all over my body--not through the medium of his device. He closed-in on me that day we left, and I was shocked by the electrodes and knocked unconscious. Somehow, he managed to keep me in that state for the entire journey. When I awoke, we were entering the orbit of Xyla and your planet was visible just out the window."

"How were you so sure that I wouldn't just kill you just now? Don't tell me that you are immune to the *pthatomyzer* as well?"

"Naturally, a man can never be one-hundred percent sure what any woman might do in any given situation. Just a bit ago, you told me that the Xylan scientists had a million questions for me. That made it a fair bet that you would wish to render me unconscious-- not into a gaseous state. And if you were going to knock me out, I reasoned that you would revert to the long-term *comapthyzer* setting versus the shorter-term *somnipthyzer*. That way you wouldn't have to worry about me waking up and becoming a nuisance until long after you were able to reach Xyla."

The girl's chin raised in defiance. Her gaze was brave and unflinching and again Bru was impressed by her otherworldly beauty.   1

"What will you do now?" she asked.

There may have been a hint of regret on Bru's face when he tapped the small button on his device and released a stream of *comapthyzer* energy upon the girl--but only a hint. He immediately reached for her weakening form and caught her beneath her arms as she collapsed, pulling her to him so that she didn't suffer a hard fall to the cabin floor. She didn't resist, but instead leaned into the man, with the remnants of one of those enticing smiles of hers partially visible on her face; he continued to support her when her legs completely went out from under her.

***

While Penelephii snoozed in a reclining seat in which she was safely strapped, Bru finished the input of some final settings on the navigation console. Having given her a dose of the *comapthyzer*--the same ray he had used on the sorcerer in the Xylan council chamber--he knew that she would slumber all the way to Xyla. He finished up what he was doing and prepared to exit the vessel.

Part of Bru loathed to part with the ship. It offered him a form of freedom that would never again be his. He'd pondered leaving it to be destroyed by the volcano and even considered hiding it away somewhere safe for his later use; it would have been nice to have taken Oona on flights until the fuel bars were expended. Not that he couldn't create new ones; of course, he could. No matter; it must go to serve another purpose.

He took a last look about the command cabin. Spotting Penelephii's device where she had dropped it to the floor, he pocketed it as well; she wouldn't be needing it. Sealing his Xylan all-weather suit against the frigid cold that awaited him the instant he stepped outside the ship, he proceeded down the ramp and stepped onto the stony ledge below the crater rim.

Sighing, he issued the command to shut and seal the door. He had set the ship on a timed takeoff and that time was rapidly approaching. With the advent of the Xylan girl into the mix, he had decided he could no longer allow the ship to be vaporized in the forthcoming detonation, nor might he keep it. Instead, he would use it to send Penelephii home.

His preparations complete, the hunter proceeded straight to the *pthellow* storage chest where Draugra had supposedly left Oona's necklace.

"It better be here, Draugra," he threatened, squatting before the chest.

Bru grunted with satisfaction when he saw the necklace lying in the first tray he opened. There were a few other things there that he remembered having on his person when he set out from the tribe the day he was banished; his stone knife wasn't among them.

"*Pthakker*," he grumbled. "He probably ditched it after he blasted me. No matter. I have his device. *Pthell*'s teeth! It's lucky for him that, with wisdom, I became a congenial man no longer strictly governed by my emotions or I'd have fried his *pthazz* for real."

Most of the other things in the storage container he left where they lay; they no longer seemed as important as they once had. He then proceeded to the entrance to the ice cavern where he had been tortured into becoming a genius who repaired a starship for a man from another galaxy.

Outside in the freezing temperatures of the mountainous elevations, he turned his head in time to see Draugra's Z2, set on *phautomatic*, lift up and angle away on its return voyage to Xyla. Its trajectory was away from him, so he didn't get to see it split the heavens and disappear into the sky because of the vertical heights of the sheer faces of The Fang of Tysk looming over him. He started down a rocky trail, one he presumed Draugra utilized when foraging for hillmen to use in his instructor-helm experiments prior to capturing Bru.

Just beyond the entrance to the ice cavern, frozen solid, were the bodies of several of these. Bru's face darkened when he spotted their misshapen forms. "They're the enemy of my people," he mused, "yet they did not deserve to die like this. Poor, dumb *phebühstahrts*."

Bru proceeded to climb downwards. At one point in time, a descent such as this would have taxed his courage to its uttermost. However, after his experiences since falling into the sorcerer's hands he now no longer feared mountain heights. How could he-- one who had hovered miles above two worlds?

1

"I guess I have him to thank for that at least," the man admitted. He spoke aloud just to hear something other than the volcanic grumbles in the stone and the roar of icy winds.

The further down the treacherous path he descended, the more bodies he discovered, tumbled from above. Dozens had become tightly jammed, one upon another, in a deep crevice where Draugra had been tossing them unceremoniously over the edge from the ice cavern. Bru shook his head in disgust and pity at sight of their wretched, mangled bodies and wondered how many more had fallen the remainder of the great heights to the rocky feet of the mountain.

No matter how careful he was Bru still had several close calls that left him dangling over precipitous heights; he was, after all, an inexperienced climber. At least he wasn't freezing, however, which would have been the case had he been clothed only in the animal furs customary of his people. The temperatures here were sub-freezing, if the frost covering the stone was any indication; but the futuristic clothing of Xyla kept him warm and comfortable to his furthest extremities.

When his feet finally found level ground, he was relieved even if he hated to admit it; he almost thanked Lyra, *pthak* her. He was in a narrow defile which appeared would open onto the plains east of the lake. Shortly, he recognized where he was; it was the same canyon in which he had discovered the remains of 'Tysk beneath the rock fall, and in which he had hidden from the group of hillmen. It had also been here that he had fallen prey to Draugra's sleep-inducing *somnipthyzer* that had left him reeling and finally, unconscious.

Bru paused at the collapsed stone where the now-scattered, skeletal remains of Tysk were still visible. Months had passed, and eaters of carrion had by now picked the cat's bones clean. Bru shrugged. He had been thinking about the situation of Gla and the tiger head, and of the price Ra had set to mate with his daughter. With the aid of his newfound knowledge he had arrived at a conclusion that before he would have found intellectually impossible to have considered.

"Ra set the price for Oona as the skull of Tysk," he mused philosophically. "However, Ra never said that one had to kill the tiger; only bring him its skull. And Gla did that, the *pthakker*! That's all Ra cared about. I suppose Gla won her *phair* and square, as much as I hate to admit it. It doesn't make it any easier to bear, however. And I'm still going to punch him in the face for being a *pthakking* liar."

Also present on the ground were bits of mostly-disintegrated human remains--all that was left of the hillmen Draugra had wiped out with his *pthatomyzer* when they had suddenly returned. Several intact stone knives and spears were also lying upon the broken stone of the canyon because the Xylan disintegrator acts only upon living organic material.

Since his knife had been missing from the storage chest, he looked for it here and at last found it where Draugra had apparently discarded it. The hunter also availed himself of one of the hillmens' spears, more out of habit than from necessity; Bru felt the most at home when he had a stone knife thrust through a skin strap tied around his waist and a heavy, stone-tipped spear gripped in his meaty ham fists.

Having pockets full of meal rations which were tiny cylinders consisting of a super concentration of the necessary proteins and minerals to provide energy, health and sustenance, and being warm and comfortable in his Xylan outfit, and completely unworried since he had both Draugra's and Penelephii's devices in his pockets, his hike was undertaken with an ease, comfort and sense of security he had never before experienced when walking the wilds of his savage, primordial world.

The attack happened before he became aware it had even begun. His sense of alertness had become numbed with the association of the Xylans who live in safe cities far above the ground. Sealed in his pockets on either hand were the futuristic, Xylan devices that could render a monstrous beast into a barely-visible cloud of atoms that would then drift away on the lightest breeze. But when fractions of moments are all one has in which to react, unzipping a pocket and preparing a device for use *on the correct setting* would seem to take an eternity.

1

16

Thus it was the spear that Bru bore familiarly in his strong hands with which he met the flying body of Tysk who had launched from a height of several *pheet* above Bru's head where he had lain in wait on a jumble of rock that lay south of the lake. Prior to his experiences with Draugra and the other Xylans, Bru would have kept a wary eye peeled for this very scenario; yet today he had been surprised by the sound of the roar that Tysk only released in mid-flight after the great cat was sure of its prey.

Lyra alone knows how he managed to bring the tip of the spear up so quickly. There was no time to aim his thrust. His reaction was a rudimentary form of instinctual movement at its most base level. The tip of his spear tore into flesh, and a huge, tawny mass slammed into him. Bru's head rebounded from the hard, stony soil beneath the heavy form of the beast, and he knew no more.

24. Kusk, the Bear

Bru awakened to the sounds of huffing and grunting, and to a sensation as of something extremely heavy lying upon him--heavy, and strong smelling. It was the movement of this heavy mass being violently disturbed, as though someone were attempting to drag the great weight off of him, that had jostled him awake. The body of Tysk! It must be what was lying on top of him. So, he had slain the great cat; it followed suit, then, that the plainsmen--his people--had discovered him. They must even now be attempting to remove the heavy body to free him.

One of his arms had become trapped along his side beneath the tiger; beneath the hand on this side he could feel the solid form of Penelephii's device where it lay, sealed in a pocket. The man was still struggling to come to his senses, but it only took a single glimpse of an enormous, hairy, claw-tipped paw as viewed from his position beneath Tysk's corpse to assure him this was not his people trying to rescue him. Instead, this was Kusk, the bear, tearing at its meal, and working its way toward Bru's partially exposed face which it had yet to discover where he lay mostly hidden beneath the cat.

The bear continued to grunt and tear at the carcass. Bru caught the scent of blood mingling with the rancid smell of torn intestines as the bear, uncaring of whether it ate flesh or organ, tore into both indiscriminately. The body of Tysk continued to be wracked with convulsive motions, its limp, rubbery form jiggling as a result of the bear's savage actions to remove as much organic material per bite as possible and gulp it down its capacious maw before a mightier contender was to stumble upon its fortuitous find and steal it; Bru somehow doubted that such existed.

It must have been that some frenzied effort on Bru's part to free his device alerted the bear that something unusual was taking place beneath the tiger's dead body. Perhaps it was the sound it heard when the hunter unsealed the pocket wherein lay Penelephii's device that caught its attention? Lyra, he was thankful he'd decided to keep her device along with Draugra's, and that he had placed one of them in each of his front pockets. He could never have   1 reached Draugra's device, which lay upon his other side with the tiger's form completely blocking access to it; that arm was hopelessly pinioned.

Now Kusk began sniffing his meal more closely and discovered much to his delight that a tasty appetizer in the form of a living man awaited his rapacious appetite and epicurean palate. The subsequent roar that this realization invoked nearly deafened the hunter. Becoming frantic now that he had been discovered, the man tugged upon the device which had become snared in the soft, Xylan pocket lining. His movement was seriously hampered, of course, by the tiger's ponderous corpse; and now the bear was clawing at the tiger's limp form beneath which Bru attempted to burrow even further.

The device felt like it was beginning to work free of the pocket lining but by now the bear had went around to Tysk's other side and began hauling upon the tiger's corpse from that side in an attempt to roll it off of Bru's form. It was determined to reach the man one way or another. And in this the man saw that the giant cave bear was going to be successful. Initially the beast had been content to tear out great bites of tiger flesh, but now that it knew of this tasty tidbit it was intent to come at the living succulence hiding beneath Tysk; it could always eat the tiger later.

Although Bru couldn't possibly be aware of it, nothing is tastier to Kusk than eating the flesh of a living man. Their prey can scream all it wants in its pure agony and frightful terror; it matters not to a bear. To Kusk, man tastes best when his living blood is pumping hot and red into its mouth, even if this lasts only for a short duration before the victim expires.

With the certainty of inevitability, Tysk's body finally rolled limply over, exposing the man underneath it. In the same instant that mighty Kusk clambered over the carcass to get at the tasty plainsman, Bru was at last able to free the Xylan device from his pocket where it was snared.

He worked the setting frantically, being unsure of which setting exactly it landed upon; for all he knew, when he pressed its button the device would try to unlock Draugra's apartment back on Xyla.

Bringing it up in feverish haste, he let the bear have it full in the face--and was relieved when the *pthatomyzer* ray turned the front half of the monster into a sticky and gruesome red cloud. The back half of the body collapsed instantly and heavily upon the corpse of the tiger whose fur became drenched in the dead bear's crimson flow.

***

Far, far away--much farther away than any plainsman of Bru's world would have found possible to have imagined or conceived--Penelephii awakened. She was sitting in Draugra's ship where she had been securely strapped into a reclining chair in the cabin. Visible out the front viewscreen was a scene she immediately recognized--it was the landing bay of Draugra's flat.

As she realized the trick that Bru had played upon her, she cursed. To further sour her mood, Draugra chose that moment to step into the docking bay. Instantly spotting her face in the window, he grinned and began leering lecherously, causing her stomach to roll.

She reached for her device, but it was not to be found. Bru again! Furious, she began rapidly tapping on the navigation console. No matter; she would play it off that Bru had kidnapped her--but she had only moments to act. She would send the spatial coordinates of the savage's homeworld to her own vessel's navigation system and then erase them from Draugra's. He would know she had done it, of course; but it would do him no good. It was as she began frantically following the familiar screens that a sudden truth dawned upon her.

"That *pthakking pthakker*! He reprogrammed the navigation system to erase all history en route. The memory banks, including all of the backups, are wiped clean! We may never find that planet again!"

The girl's characteristic aplomb began evaporating when she heard the door of the ship open and the hum of the boarding ramp lowering to the landing bay floor. A commotion in the bay attracted her attention; others were arriving.

"Who the *Pthell* now?" she griped.

1

Undoubtedly, the vessel's incoming trajectory had been tracked, and then security forces summoned after its destination had become realized. They had probably been looking constantly and everywhere for this ship.

At the same moment that Draugra boarded his vessel and greeted his former lover who was sitting in the command console, a recording started playing *pthautomatically* that captured both their attention and the attention of those newly arrived. Cast upon the floor of the landing bay where it was visible to all was a *pthologram* of hers' and Bru's last encounter which had taken place in the control cabin on the hunter's homeworld. While it played, security troops stormed onto the vessel as more continued to pour into the landing bay.

Bru's original intention had been to trigger a random *pthologram* recording to distract Penelephii when she had accosted him in the control cabin; instead, reaching behind him to the controls blindly, he had accidentally tapped the Record button. After reprogramming the navigation *comphuter* to erase all of the navigation data enroute and discovering the recording, he had set up the equipment to play it *pthautomatically* upon detecting Draugra's voice pattern. Grinning, he had almost wished he could be there to see it.

With a crestfallen appearance, Pylapharum watched the three-dimensional recording of Penelephii tempting Bru and uttering her complete and utter disdain for Draugra and himself.

"*Pylapharum? That fool? He doesn't have the grit,*" echoed the *pthologram* version of the girl. "*And Draugra can't be trusted. Now a man like you, Bru...*"

By this time the security force was leading the girl from the vessel for questioning, with Draugra following and looking as innocent as possible.

"Take that man also." His face dark, Pylapharum stabbed a condemning finger at Draugra; but he refused to look at Penelephii.

"What? Me? You're insane!" the sorcerer objected.

"No, I am not." He turned to the *phaptain* of the security contingent. "That is the man who disintegrated Councilman Phylbyr in the council room."

"You back-stabbing *phebiistart*!" Draugra roared.

"It seems I've let the *pthat* out of the bag," Pylapharum retorted coolly. "Sorry if I hit a nerve, Drauggy old boy."

News of the arrival of Draugra's vessel had reached the ears of the entire council by this time and now these began filing into the landing bay. Greed for the return of the vessel containing the coordinates of the wonderful new world Draugra had discovered-- and of Bru, his creation--played across their faces like the reflections of a campfire dancing across the features of a savage.

The *phaptain* of the security detail signaled to two of his men to see to Draugra. With a sweeping glance, Pylapharum took in the members of the council who were in a state of confusion upon seeing the security forces taking Draugra and Penelephii into custody.

"What is the meaning of this?" demanded the chairman. He strode truculently up to Pylapharum and the *phaptain*.

The chairman had long since perfected an imperious tone which he used to undermine and destroy the confidence of others. The *phaptain* glanced at Pylapharum doubtfully.

"You and the entire council stand accused," Pylapharum explained. Nodding at the *phaptain*, he gestured at all of them. The man nodded resolutely and signaled to a squad of troopers who swarmed the group of protesting scientists.

"This man--Draugra--is most likely guilty of killing a man who went missing two years ago--a man by the name of Krahktohl," Pylapharum continued. "The entire council supported Draugra's effort in the name of science. Each of them stood idly by while he slaughtered Councilman Phylbyr who alone--other than me--dared to raise an objection."

"He lies!" shrieked Chrysii; her voice was tinged with desperation. She looked for Phlibion, but he was already face-first against a wall with two troopers standing behind him; one of these was slipping a device about the young councilman's wrists.

1

22

The security forces began herding the other council members against the same stretch of wall but hesitated when the council chairman, one of the most powerful figures on the planet and not one to anger lightly, halted them with a raised hand.

"He is a madman--" he began, with one, shaking hand pointing weakly at Pylapharum.

"Am I?" roared Pylapharum, becoming angry himself. "Perhaps you have forgotten, chairman, the *pthologram* recordings which are *pthautomatically* triggered during all sessions."

"Sweet Lyra!" a stressed councilman swore.

The chairman only smiled smugly. "You are referring, I presume, to the recordings which were accidentally erased on the same day Draugra's ship was commandeered?"

"Praise Lyra!" the same councilman beamed, relieved.

Now it was Pylapharum's turn to gloat. "No, not those recordings, chairman. Sweet dear Lyra--you *phoron*! *Of course, I knew you would erase them*! *Phidiot*! I was referring to the copies I saved to my device and sent to security headquarters while the lot of you rushed after the savage once we forced the door locks he'd sabotaged. I lingered long enough to make those backups because, ladies and *phentlemen* of the council--you are not as brilliant as you have deluded yourselves into thinking, but instead you are rather predictable."

Withdrawing his device to the quick intakes of breath by the various council members nearby, Pylapharum spoke a command into it and was rewarded with a life-sized *pthologram* of the gruesome scene with which they were all familiar. The chairman staggered and his face turned ashen, as did those of the other members of the council.

Recovering, the chairman gasped, "You *pthakking* upstart! You'll never sit on the council, Pylapharum! I can see to that from within an internment chamber, by Lyra!"

Pylapharum didn't resist the smile that followed the chairman's threat. "How does it feel, councilman, to have been bested and outmaneuvered by a neophyte, and a stone age savage?"

Pylapharum's smile was short-lived, however; when he turned his head and looked at Penelephii, his expression became bitter with regret.

"Come on, you!" growled the *phaptain*; and he shoved the chairman's face into the stone wall and snapped a restraint about his wrists.

***

Bru dusted off and adjusted his device so that it would be easier to access if he needed it quickly in the future. Somewhat ruefully, he eyed the mauled and partially-devoured body of Tysk. It was too late to be the first to bring a tiger head to Ra, but at least he had slain this one with his own hands--unlike Gla. And, Bru had done so with a spear--not with one of the two Xylan devices he possessed--which made him even happier.

"Oh, what the *Pthell*!" he muttered.

Taking out one of the devices he made a minute adjustment to its settings, causing a cutting beam narrower than a fine hair to extend a short distance from the device. Being careful to not pass this beam near his own body or extremities, he used it to neatly slice the head from the body of Tysk.

"Hmph!" he grunted. Eyeing the device as the meaty head fell away from Tysk's shoulders, he said, "I wish the *Pthell* I'd had this thing a long time ago. I could carve Moosh up in a trice with this."

It took the hunter an hour or so to rig up a drag sled of felled saplings and grasses to bear the heavy head, but he felt the effort to be worth the time invested. His Xylan device was an immense help to him. Cutting down small saplings with a finely dialed cutting beam was nothing and took only a heartbeat to accomplish. Braiding the grasses to tie the trees together? Well, that just took what it took.

Bru had high hopes that the gift of a second tiger head--one that had been taken in a good, honest challenge--might help him gain back the respect of tribe and--more importantly--the good graces of Ra.

"I've hunted with Ra; maybe he has cooled down and will now listen to reason. I will explain to him that I was out of my head in love with his daughter; that I couldn't imagine a life without her. I also can't imagine her mated to a spineless *phwimp* like Gla. If we're attacked by hillmen, it is *she* who would have to protect *him*, by Kusk. And she could do it, too!"

Thinking about the bear caused him to glance at the hideous remains of Kusk lying beside the tiger.

"This sort of technology must be doled out in tiny portions to the people," he muttered. "I, myself--as hotheaded as I once was--if I'd possessed a device like this, Gla might be dead right now." Having made up his mind, he unclipped the device from his side and--although it entailed taking greater risk--slipped it into a pouch where it would be out of sight.

25. Oona

Bru stood gazing for several moments at the collection of tents sitting out upon the plains, his heart swelling with emotion. They had not budged a *phinch* since he had left. Even in the face of the smoke and ground tremors, they were still here. They were a simple people; the angry mountains were, to them, very far away although in reality they were less than a day's walk and lay, he knew, in quite deadly proximity.

Striding into the midst of the shelters of the Tribe of the Seven Rivers Bru felt happier than he recalled feeling in months. He could scarcely believe he was back among his people whom he had nearly given up hope of ever again seeing.

Bru had temporarily forgotten that he had been banished until he walked into the encampment. He realized then that the possibility existed that his people might not allow him to return; no matter. If they wished him to leave again, he would leave--but not before he convinced them that they, too, must vacate this place and flee to a point of safety. This he deemed to be at least fifty *phmiles* southwest which would place them at an elevation above the pyroclastic flow and mud slides, and beyond the reach of the tons of rocky shrapnel that would be unleashed in every direction together with the evaporating lake and rivers.

Realizing that his foreign garb might confuse people and recalling that it had frightened him the first time he saw Draugra wearing it, he threw back the hood and the breathing apparatus which had protected his lungs from the sub-zero temperatures of the mountain heights. The suit was a handy contraption, he'd found, that kept the body comfortable no matter the outside temperature fluctuations. But being late afternoon on the plains he found the weather to be quite comfortable. With the Xylan garb on, he hadn't even noticed how warm it was until he removed the hood.

"Who you?"

The voice was that of Skarf. Bru grinned; as gruff as was Skarf he was still glad to see the man.

1

26

"I am Bru," he rejoined, slipping naturally into the vernacular of the tribe.

"Bru? You not Bru! Who you?" Skarf demanded again nervously. "Why you here? You hill man? Skarf kill!"

Others began to gather, exiting their hide tents where they had most likely retreated following an afternoon meal. Bru sighed. How he had missed these people!

"I am Bru! Bru has come to save the tribe," he grunted and motioned calmly.

"Bru no good!" It was Prud; the fuel-gatherer had arrived. "Bru can't save tribe!"

Prud grimaced, causing the fickle crowd to mimic him; everyone frowned.

This was not going how Bru had hoped. He needed to speak to someone who spoke with the voice of wisdom and sense.

"Prud stupid; Bru will talk to Ra. Where is Ra?"

Several muttered under their breath, but none replied with anything definite that Bru could make out clearly. There was a disturbance and the crowd parted; Oona made her way forward. At first all Bru saw was the great beauty of the girl's face. How much more lovely she was than the sophisticated Penelephii or Chrysii.

The next thing he saw was her rounded belly; the girl was with child.

Bru's expression crumbled. He had been gone longer than he had imagined. How had he forgotten? Oona was to be mated with Gla upon the Wyrm Moon; that time had long come and gone. As the girl came forward, the plainspeople parted before her. And as she passed each one their heads dropped, and they muttered murmurings which Bru could not quite make out. After an eternity, she paused before him.

"You are truly Bru?" The girl searched his face piercingly, as if longing--no, needing--for it to be him.

He had seen his image in the polished glass surfaces the Xylans called *phirrors*, and in the reflective panels on ships and buildings. He had stared at his own reflection in the viewscreen of a starship with a planet visible beyond it, and he had seen it in the surface of the little rills and creeks he passed while making his way here from the mountains. He knew he was changed. The experiments he had undergone had subtly revised his features.

Alright, he admitted, *it goes beyond subtlety. I look pthakking different.*

"Oona, it is I," he said, feeling ashamed.

Oona continued to gaze upon him. The longer she looked at him, the more nervous the man became, fearing that she might not like what she saw. After a few tense moments, however, she beamed.

"You are Bru! Oona sees Bru, now!" The girl turned to those gathered behind her and smiled. "This is Bru! Bru has returned!"

Unsurprisingly, Prud was not thrilled. But many of the others seemed happy by his return. Bru now learned of a catastrophe that had overcome the tribe the night of the Wyrm Moon, the night Oona was to be officially mated to Gla.

"Many Moosh stampede," explained Skarf, pointing toward the distant lake; Skarf, too, had finally recognized his fellow hunter. The animated plainsman spread his arms wide as he indicated the size of the herd. "Moosh trample Ra's shelter. Gla was with Ra. Chief was smashed! Gla was smashed!"

Bru nodded his head. It made sense. The animals were sensitive to the increased seismic activity which his people were ignoring, thinking themselves safe due to the distance to the mountains. He had to shake his head at the wisdom of animals as compared to that of creatures who were supposed to have more highly developed reasoning faculties. The people simply had no idea how far reaching that destructive forces of this nature could be.

Many now took note of Bru's sled which he had dragged into the camp, and the immense tiger head that was tied to it with woven grasses.

"A fine head!" beamed Skarf, grinning straight at Prud.

Others gathered around to ooh and awe the trophy. It was obviously a fresh kill, and that of a beast in its prime.

"Bru killed Tysk with his spear," Bru boasted. He held the spear aloft, which he had removed from the tiger's body. It was slathered in gore for a third of its length. But he didn't mention Kusk as the

1

28

bear had been killed with Draugra's device, and therefor there was no honor attached to its death.

"A fresh kill! A mighty tiger!" another declared, squatting before the head. "Bru mighty hunter! Bru killed Tysk!"

Bru grinned but then turned back to Oona. So, the mammoth herd had stampeded, run amok through the tribe's encampment and slain the unfortunates in their path.

"Who else smashed?" the hunter asked her, falling back naturally into the simple language he had known all his life.

"No one," answered Oona.

Her face was sad. Bru recalled that she'd always had a good relationship with her father who had always doted on her. Despite his eviction from the tribe by Ra, Bru held no rancor against the old man. Bru had disobeyed Ra, and had suffered the consequences of his actions; he still held his chief in great respect.

But he did wonder to what extent Oona's frown was for Gla-- the father of her child. He now understood clearly where things stood. If the chief's daughter was with child and her mate was killed, then the unborn child, if it was male, would become the next chief. If the child was female, the chief's daughter had the option of delaying until the next Wyrm Moon the choosing of a new mate who would then become chief; alternatively, she could pass and elect to have the tribe choose a new chief. Oona had not yet chosen another mate to become chief, so the tribe awaited the birth of her child to see if it was male. If it was not, then she must either take a mate or she must abdicate.

During this interim, however, Oona was allowed to rule as regent. As such, she now announced to the tribe that Bru was to be allowed to remain. Given that the only ones who had any real complaint against him were dead, this decision went uncontested; quite the opposite, most were glad to welcome Bru back to the fold and nodded their heads in agreement. There were rumblings in the ground and smoke could be seen in the mountains; things were unseemly. An extra spear was very greatly needed at this crucial time to steady the tribe and provide meat following the death of their chief.

129

Only Prud and a few fire-feeders and fuel-gatherers disagreed, but their kind disliked the hunter caste who always made them feel inferior. Prud's objection came as no surprise to anyone, but after Skarf growled at them, they drifted to the back of the crowd and ceased their grumblings--at least insofar as any grumblings that might reach the ears of Skarf.

When he had the opportunity, Bru spoke with Oona alone.

"Where Bru been?" the girl asked; a woman, whether of an advanced society such as that found on Xyla, or among the simple tents of the Pleistocene, is a creature of innate curiosity.

How could he tell her that he had become the prisoner of a man from another world? And even stranger, that he had been bourn to this world himself and, although the odds had been stacked heavily against him, had been able to return home? And how could he bring himself to frighten her by revealing that the grim possibility existed that, although he had erased the stored co-ordinates to their world from the vessel's data stores, that one day another Krahktohl might rediscover their tiny planet and that on that dark day their skies might be filled with ships in their thousands from Xyla or some other, unwelcome world?

"Bru was captured by a sorcerer," he opted for, recalling Draugra's mocking words. He also recalled the weeks when Draugra placed helmet after helmet over his face, their umbilicals sliding sickeningly down his throat, the clamps over his eyes and ears, the cascade of information flowing at a disgusting rate into a mind that could barely absorb it without perishing--but somehow managed to do so.

"Bru!" Oona gasped. "No!"

"Sorcerer tortured Bru," he whispered. "Bru was made a slave; Bru labored for the sorcerer."

"And did Bru kill the sorcerer?" The girl's voice was barely a whisper.

The hunter hesitated. Sometimes he regretted not having killed Draugra. He'd had the opportunity and the weapon had been in his hand. Yet he had decided against it.

1

"No," he said. "Bru did not kill. But since the sorcerer tried to steal Bru's dreams, Bru took the sorcerer's dreams from him. What he wanted the most, Bru took away."

He was thinking of all those times he tried to conjure Oona's sweet face and form only to find his mind's eye blotted with images of Draugra's debased desires for Penelephii. But no more; *those* images he had ripped out or replaced.

The girl was quiet for a moment. "What did the bad man want?"

"Draugra wanted to enslave Bru; Draugra wanted to enslave the tribe . . . enslave Oona!"

The girl's gasp was of pure fright--to be spoken of by an evil one of such power as this man obviously had been to have captured and enslaved her mighty and beloved Bru was an ill thing. To think that this sorcerer wished to take them all captive--enslave them, torture them, perhaps kill them; she grasped Bru's hand in hers.

"But Bru learned many good things from the sorcerer," Bru continued. "Sorcerer smart--now Bru smart. Bru will teach tribe. But first, tribe follows Bru away from here."

"We will follow Bru anywhere!" the girl replied earnestly.

Bru looked down into the girl's beautiful face only to inescapably find himself staring at her pronounced belly. "Gla's son will make fine chief. Bru will hunt for Oona and the son of Oona."

Thus spoke the men of the tribe of the unborn--as though the child was predestined to be a son and spear wielder for the tribe, and a mighty hunter in the field. In essence, Bru had just sworn fealty to Oona's son if it was a male and destined to become the chief of the tribe, even in the face of the fact that this child was the son of a despised rival.

"Bru," Oona said softly. She took the man's hand and pressed it to her abdomen. He felt half inclined to resist; was this not the unborn get of his rival? He guessed she wished to rekindle their relationship now that Gla was no longer in the picture, maybe even make Bru interim chief until the child arrived--to have him assist her in raising Gla's unborn; to hunt for them.

131

"Oona?" To his own ears his voice sounded choked.

"This is Bru's son. Mighty hunter, mighty fighter." She looked up into his eyes from beneath her thick lashes. "Oona never mated with Gla. Oona only mated with Bru!"

The hunter's heart pounded in his chest, beating with a force never experienced by any plainsman, hillman or Xylan. He now understood that, although Gla had been ritualistically mated to Oona according to the rites and customs of their people, he had never consummated the union.

For he had been asked by Ra to join him in the chief's shelter immediately following the ritual where the former chief had possibly wished to discuss the details of his daughter's leaving her father's household. But neither Ra nor Gla ever again set foot outside that shelter, both having been crushed beneath the feet of a herd of frightened mammoths.

"What happen to Bru? Why Bru look so different? Bru was handsome before . . . but now Bru is beautiful!"

The girl gasped when two strong arms pulled her to him. The man *pthautomatically* switched to the Xylan language then in which he was fluent because that which he wished to say next wasn't expressible in the simple tongue of the plainsmen.

"I crossed far reaches of space, sweet Oona," he whispered. "I saw worlds and vistas that your pure eyes have never beheld and never will, Lyra willing. I've gazed on alien moons and watched the expanse of heavens fold upon itself. I've flown ships beyond the speed of light and defended our world from a galaxy of invaders, for your sweet sake. And now, I take up the mantle of chief with you and our child by my side, my little barbarian princess--beloved Oona!"

And Bru, soon to be chief of the Tribe of the Seven Rivers following the simple--but obligatory--rituals, kissed his mate upon her lips. One hand found its way around her waist and pulled her close against him, and the other caressed the soft, tanned hide covering her swollen belly. And although Oona had understood not a single word of her mighty mate's speech, she could not mistake the welcome feel of his hands, nor the warmth of his lips against her own.

1

The End

An Invitation!

Dear reader,

I hope you enjoyed this romp through the Pleistocene! I wish to extend an invitation to leave feedback for this story in the form of a review should you be so inclined.

And if you liked this story you might be interested in my other works. Consider visiting my site for descriptions of other stories that might appeal to you. I'm always working to add to my published library, so check back from time to time for news.

Best regards,
Chris

List of Works

Currently available:

- The Valley of Despair (Tales of Despair Vol I)
- The Cosmos of Despair (Tales of Despair Vol II)
- On A Winter's Eve
- The Treasure of Akram el-Amin
- The Blonde Goddess of Tikka-Tikka (Tales of the Tomahawk Vol I)
- The Banshee of the Atacama (Tales of the Tomahawk Vol II)
- Atlas of the Serpent Men (A Tale of Conan of Cimmeria)
- Conan and Old Crem (A Tale of Conan of Cimmeria)
- The Hunter and the Sorcerer (Prehistoric Tales Vol I)

Coming next:

- The Savage from Atlantis (Prehistoric Tales Vol II)
- Untitled (Tales of the Tomahawk Vol III)

1

Acknowledgements

I wish to extend my heartfelt gratitude to my wife who listens as I go on and on about my stories. I know she must sometimes tire of hearing about plots and characters, but she always listens. Thanks, honey.

I wish to express my gratitude to my friend, Scott, with whom I share many common interests. As such, we frequently talk about stories. He has helped me through writing several novels set on the Barsoom of Edgar Rice Burroughs which are under contract with ERB Inc., and a host of short stories, offering his sage advice along the way.

After reading their stories for years I must acknowledge the fine authors who influenced me from beyond (for many of them have sailed the Darkling Sea, as McKiernan would say) to give something back to the rich world of well-spun tales I've enjoyed since I was a youth.

I would like to thank fellow authors Gilbert M. Stack and William L. Hahn for their invaluable insight and advice. Their gift of proofreading the early drafts of this novel really paid dividends. I feel the story is so much the better for their insightful questions and frank comments. Thanks, guys, really.

I also wish to thank God for giving me whatever it is that drives me to write stories. I just have one favor to ask: keep 'em coming

About the Author

Chris spent years playing guitar in and out of bands and was, during that time, more of a voracious reader than a writer. After that last band collapsed, he turned from writing songs to writing stories, eventually turning out a half million-word Barsoom series as a tribute to Edgar Rice Burroughs (currently under contract to ERB Inc.) and a host of self-published short stories and poems.

Something inside drives him to create, and so together with writing and playing guitar, he also dabbles in painting (the cover for his novel, *The Hunter and the Sorcerer*, is one of his).

You may find him on his website *ChrisLAdamsBizarreTales.com*. There, you'll find links, information on available stories, and other things you might find of interest.

Chris enjoys talking about favorite authors, writing and collecting books so feel free to shoot him an email from his Contact page.

Chris resides in Southern West Virginia with his wife and two children.

Bizarre Tales

To keep up with Chris, check out the Bizarre Tales blog on GoodReads at:

https://www.goodreads.com/author/show/15259542.Chris_L_Adams/blog

Or, visit the Bizarre Tales website at *ChrisLAdamsBizarreTales.com* where you will find fantasy paintings, B&W colorizations, News and Items of Notes and many various things with which Chris becomes involved.

1

And remember to look for the Bizarre Tales Logo © on the cover!

Manufactured by Amazon.ca
Bolton, ON